Blooming

AT THE
TEXAS SUNRISE
MOTEL

Blooming

AT THE
TEXAS SUNRISE
MOTEL

KIMBERLY WILLIS HOLT

Christy Ottaviano Books
Henry Holt and Company
New York

Henry Holt and Company, *Publishers since 1866*
175 Fifth Avenue, New York, New York 10010 • mackids.com

Henry Holt® is a registered trademark of Macmillan Publishing Group, LLC.
Text copyright © 2017 by Kimberly Willis Holt
Illustrations copyright © 2017 by Vera Rosenberry
All rights reserved.

Library of Congress Cataloging-in-Publication Data
Names: Holt, Kimberly Willis, author.
Title: Blooming at the Texas Sunrise Motel / Kimberly Willis Holt.
Description: First edition. | New York : Henry Holt and Company, [2017]. |
"Christy Ottaviano Books." | Summary: After the sudden death of her parents,
Stevie, thirteen, is sent to live at a rundown motel, where she charms everyone
except her estranged grandfather.
Identifiers: LCCN 2016027032 (print) | LCCN 2016054961 (ebook) | ISBN 9781627793247
(hardback) | ISBN 9781627793254 (ebook)
Subjects: | CYAC: Grandfathers—Fiction. | Grief—Fiction. | Hotels, motels, etc.—Fiction.
| Orphans—Fiction. | Gardens—Fiction. | BISAC: JUVENILE FICTION / Family /
Orphans & Foster Homes. | JUVENILE FICTION / Social Issues / Friendship. |
JUVENILE FICTION / Social Issues / Values & Virtues.
Classification: LCC PZ7.H74023 Blo 2017 (print) | LCC PZ7.H74023 (ebook) |
DDC [Fic]—dc23
LC record available at https://lccn.loc.gov/2016027032

Our books may be purchased in bulk for promotional, educational,
or business use. Please contact your local bookseller or the
Macmillan Corporate and Premium Sales Department at (800) 221-7945 ext. 5442
or by e-mail at MacmillanSpecialMarkets@macmillan.com.

First edition—2017 / Designed by Patrick Collins
Printed in the United States of America by LSC Communications,
Harrisonburg, Virginia

1   3   5   7   9   10   8   6   4   2

This story is for Shannon Renee Holt
and her dreams.
May they all come true.

Blooming

AT THE
TEXAS SUNRISE
MOTEL

Seedling

A plant that emerges from seed
with roots, a stem, and leaves

Chapter One

MY NAME, STEVIE GRACE, was tattooed inside a giant sun on my dad's back. Because, he said, after I was born he'd have sunshine for the rest of his days. I loved my dad's tattoos—they told the story of his life. A Louisiana shrimp boat on his right shoulder for a job he once had, and a blue backpack along his forearm for a walk across the country. The broken hoe above his left pec was easy to figure out. We had a small farm.

A daisy emerging from a tornado hung over his heart, for Mom. Ever since I was little, he'd told me a story about how Mom was swept up into a Texas tornado and landed on his doorstep. "Even with all the leaves sticking to her hair, she was the prettiest thing I'd ever seen." When I got older, I realized his story wasn't true, but I liked fairy tales. I wanted to believe it. So I never asked how they really met.

When I pointed to the rectangle-with-wing tattoo on his arm, he'd say, "That story will have to wait until you're older." Tattoos covered most of his upper body, from his neck down to his belly button. He said he'd eventually make it to his toes but he still had a lot of living to do.

I think about that now as I leave Albuquerque on a Greyhound bus, watching a lady next to me knit. Her fingers slip the red yarn over the needles at such a quick speed, it makes me dizzy to watch. Still, I can't help it. I'm mesmerized. *Down, over, and up. Down, over, and up.* The *tink-tink* sound of the needles touching. Each new stitch precisely like the last. If only my life could be as sure as her stitches.

WE LIVED IN AN ABANDONED CHURCH outside Taos, New Mexico. It was a little stucco building with a pitched tin roof and a steeple piercing purple sky. My dad called our home the Rockasita because records always played on Mom's old turntable.

Both my parents listened to old music. Dad preferred

his songs rough, like the Stones and Johnny Cash (pre–June Carter). He called Mom's music "bubblegum pop" because she liked Neil Sedaka, Barry Manilow, and the Go-Go's. Fleetwood Mac and the Beatles were the only bands they agreed on. I guess it's no wonder my parents named me after Stevie Nicks.

We may have lived in a church building, but we didn't attend services. Mom believed God was everywhere—in the wind's whisper blowing through the Red River aspens, in a single ripple on the Rio Grande, and even in the toothless grin of our neighbor Angelina Cruz. My dad agreed. And so did I.

Our home was a few miles away from Taos Plaza, right off Highway 64. A lot of cars used this route because it climbed through the Sangre de Cristo Mountains. My parents set their fruit-and-flower stand in the shade of two old plum trees that grew at the edge of the road. We called them the sweetheart trees because their branches had spread so wide, they intertwined. They never failed to provide us with enough plums to eat and sell.

Our garden put food on the table, but I hated the watering, the weeding, the planting. Sometimes I climbed one of the sweetheart trees to escape my chores. I'd hide up there on a high branch, breathing in all that sweetness and staring down at my dad's scalp.

Unfortunately, the trees were located just before a short twist along the highway, which created a sort of optical illusion. Sometimes drivers thought they were about to crash into them. The third time a driver swerved, lost control, and almost hit the trees, Dad took an axe and cut them down. Mom and I cried, but she said, "Your dad was right. They grew too close to the curve, and they're probably causing some of the accidents. What if *you*'d been in one of the trees?"

That was last summer. A month ago, I noticed a small seedling had sprouted in the spot where the two trees had grown. If they noticed, Mom and Dad didn't mention it. Accidents still happened. None of them were that serious, but whenever we saw a wreck, Mom and I would say a quick prayer. Maybe our prayers didn't make any difference, but I felt better. I liked our way of going to church because we didn't have to enter a building to worship. The opportunity could be found in every moment.

I believe this. Even after what happened.

Two weeks ago, while I was at school, a drunk driver crashed into my parents' stand. The paramedics drove my parents to the hospital. They were dead on arrival. Then they were driven to the morgue. All this happened between lunch and the end of eighth-grade geography class. I lost my parents while my teacher discussed major cities in Australia. And here's the weird thing: I was thinking about them during that lesson. Dad and Mom had said if they ever left New Mexico, Australia seemed like the kind of place they'd want to call home. We even threw our change in an empty jar that had a label with AUSTRALIA written across it. We were planning to travel there one day.

"I always fancied myself a kangaroo," Dad told us.

I burst into giggles, then announced, "I'm more of a koala bear."

Mom claimed we were both crazy. "I'm going as a photographer. I'll be sure and take your pictures, though." Then she added, "Click, click." She did that whenever her camera wasn't handy and she saw a perfect picture op.

That's what I was thinking about when my parents were dying. Maybe my parents were there with me in geography class. Maybe they were saying good-bye.

Four hours out of Albuquerque, the bus meets the Amarillo city limits. We're still a long way from the Dallas bus station. I search outside the wide window for anything resembling my home. The land is as flat as a tortilla, and the sky touches the horizon far and wide. We pass the small downtown skyline, which is more midrise than high. Right before we leave the city limits, I notice a giant cowboy statue in front of a yellow building. Mom would have taken a picture of that. I reach inside my tote bag for her camera, but it's too late. We've passed the restaurant. I twist around and watch as the cowboy becomes a matchstick. *Click, click. So this is Texas.*

I'm on my way to my grandfather's home, the Texas Sunrise Motel in Little Esther. All I know about Little Esther is that it's somewhere south of Dallas. All I know about him is that he's my mother's father and I thought he was dead. When I was little, I asked about my grandparents. Most of my friends lived near theirs, and I felt left out. Dad took me aside and said, "My family has been gone a long time now, and it's best you don't ask your mom about hers. It will make her sad." Soon after that, I caught Mom crying when a church hymn was playing on the radio. The only other song that made her cry like that was "Blackbird" by the Beatles. When she saw me watching her that day, she wiped her eyes with the back of her hand. "I'm okay. I was just remembering how my mom used to sing that song. I miss her." Because of that and what Dad had told me, I assumed her parents were dead too.

Dad and Mom talked to me about everything and anything, except their families. Winston Himmel is the closest relative I have. The only thing my dad had said about my grandfather was "He didn't like the likes of me."

And now I'm wondering, how could I ever like the likes of him?

Chapter Two

Two weeks ago, when I was asked to go to the principal's office, my best friend, Carmen, had led the class in razzing me. "Aw, someone's in trouble." I knew I wasn't. The entire walk down the hall, I wondered if Principal Sanchez was going to try again to convince me to run for student body president next year. "You're mature," she'd said the week before. "You will be a good influence on the students." I wanted to say, *Don't you know my best friend is Carmen Montoya?* Carmen skipped school more than anyone.

But when I opened the office door, everyone stopped whispering and their heads turned toward Principal Sanchez. She was standing outside her office, wearing the green suit with the blouse that tied in a bow at her neck. She looked at me with a weak smile. Her eyes were red. I remember thinking, *She must have a bad allergy. Maybe she's allergic to those wildflowers. They're blooming early this year.*

Principal Sanchez held her right arm out to me, and when I reached her, she pulled me to her side and guided me into her office. Then she closed the door.

When she told me what had happened, I didn't cry. And I didn't cry when my parents' best friend, Paco, and his new girlfriend, Sandra, picked me up and took me to their home. Nor at the funeral two days later. Whenever the priest said "Sheppard and Daisy Tanner," it didn't seem real. We'd never been in the chapel. Paco suggested it because that's where he did all his confessing. I didn't cry, because what had happened didn't seem true. But that night when I went to sleep in Paco and Sandra's spare room, I learned that if you scream into a pillow, no one can hear you.

OUR BUS DRIVER increases his speed. We can't read the billboards even if we want to. The knitting lady tells me, "I overhead the driver say he has a wedding to get to tonight."

A moment later he passes three cars on the highway outside Vernon and swerves into the right lane. We grab hold of the seat in front of us. "Must be *his* wedding," the knitting lady says.

She studies my face, her needles still clicking. I'm worried that she's going to see my sadness and ask if something's wrong and that I'll blubber to a complete stranger. Instead she asks, "How long did it take you to grow your hair that long?"

"All my life."

"It's pretty," she says. Then she looks back down at her work. It's now a rectangle so long, it forms a hill sticking out of a grocery sack at her feet.

"Is that a scarf?" I ask.

"Yes," she says, peering over her glasses. "It's for my nephew. He's over seven feet tall. He rides a unicycle. Right now he's in Baton Rouge. People don't realize it, but a Louisiana winter is cold."

"Really?"

"Yes," she says. "A wet winter can chill you to the bone."

I meant her tall nephew, not Louisiana winters. My mind wanders and I picture a giant pedaling around a city on a unicycle, a red scarf trailing in the wind behind him. Mom would have taken a picture of him for sure.

"People hire him to give out flyers. A lot of organizations want their causes known. And everyone always stops for a giant on a unicycle."

When the lady quits talking, I dig in my purse for a piece of paper. All I have is a Hershey's candy bar wrapper. I smooth it out and write, *Everyone always stops for a giant on a unicycle*. Then I tuck the note in my purse. It sounds like something I'd find in a fortune cookie.

A family of three siblings sits across the aisle from us. The big sister seems to be about ten, and her brothers look six and seven. Sometimes she puts her arm around the youngest and he leans against her, sleeping. They wear badges hanging from strings around their necks, probably with their travel information. Except for Christmastime, I'd never felt like I was missing anything not having a brother or sister. Now, watching the three of them motioning to one another at the sights outside their window, I think maybe I was.

At the station, we get off the bus and I wait for my two suitcases. Almost everything I own is inside those bags. My clothes, a few books, and the Australia jar. The only things left that I wanted were Mom's record player, albums, and photographs. Paco said he would mail them to the motel. The farm hasn't sold yet, so I have the total of my parents' closed savings account—five hundred and twelve dollars. Paco is handling the sale of the farm. There isn't a buyer, but he believes there will be soon. He says the money will bring in enough to send me to college—maybe not Harvard, but a state university. "It was a good investment," he says.

Which is really kind of funny, because my parents didn't pay one red cent for the farm. Dad won it in a chess game with a cocky rich guy from Fort Worth, who wanted to get rid of it anyway. The guy called the place "three acres of crap" because one of the neighbors lets their sheep roam on it.

"Sounded like good fertilizer to me," Dad would say. He and Mom moved to New Mexico, built a fence, and planted herbs and flowers. I was born there.

The farm is the only home I've ever had. That's why I know, all the way down to my toes, that it will wait for me.

Paco is a lawyer, but he's not like any of the lawyers on TV. He's the kind that when people can't pay with money, they pay with pigs or other livestock. He owns the farm next to ours, the one with the sheep. He brags that he didn't have to buy any of his chickens or goats. He's also who contacted my grandfather. I like Paco, but it kind of ticked me off that he knew more about my parents' past than I did. What was it they didn't want me to know?

Even though it's early, I look around for my grandfather at the station. I have no idea what he looks like, but the social worker gave him a picture of me. She also asked me to think of a secret word he could use when he met me. That way I'll know it's him. I gave her *kangaroo*. The social worker didn't say so, but I could tell she wasn't happy that my grandfather hadn't sent a picture of himself.

Right away, I see an older man dressed in a crisp white shirt and khaki pants. He smiles at me but makes no effort to walk in my direction. I wish my picture had been more recent. Paco gave the social worker one he'd taken of me with Mom and Dad. We were in front of the stand. The picture was so old, the sweetheart trees were in the background.

Now a woman with beautiful white hair joins the old man. Her mood is as sunny as her yellow sweater. She bounces in place as she points to my young bus companions. "There they are!"

The trio are with an escort, but when they see the older couple, they run toward them with outstretched arms. Their grandparents' arms aim in their direction too, reaching, reaching. They meet in a tangle of hugs and kisses. I'm happy for them, and hopeful for me.

The knitting lady waves good-bye to me as she leaves with her husband. I wish I could see her nephew wearing the red scarf. I sure hope it doesn't get stuck in a unicycle spoke.

An elderly man walks into the station. He's wearing a snug knit hat and a navy peacoat. It's April, and not hot, but too hot for a coat. He's unshaven and his clothes look shabby and dirty. He walks in my direction. When he reaches me, his stench causes me to flinch.

He moves toward me. My heart pounds. I'm already planning my getaway. I'll call Paco. I'll live with Angelina Cruz, be her caretaker. She's over a hundred years old. Then I remember. She once scared away a bear by shaking her charm bracelet in front of his face. She doesn't need me. I'll run away to an orphanage in New Mexico. They'll take me. Surely orphanages aren't that bad.

He's a few feet away now. I have no other choice: I have to make this work. I take a big breath and stand there, accepting my fate, waiting to hear the word *kangaroo*. He leans in and holds up an empty paper cup. "Can you spare some change for a bit of coffee?"

My breath leaves my body in one big *whoosh*. I'm so relieved, I dig in my pocket and give him a wrinkled dollar bill.

"Bless you, little angel," he says, and then he leaves as quickly as he came, jingling the coins in his cup. The way he walks with his back straight and head held high makes me wonder who he was and what happened to him.

ALL THE OTHER PASSENGERS on my bus have found their rides and are gone. It's only one forty-five in the afternoon, still early. I settle in a seat and open my book but catch myself reading the same paragraph over and over.

A huge clock on the back wall reads two o'clock. I shut my book and push my suitcases together.

And wait.

At two fifteen, I begin to think he won't show. After all, this isn't what he asked for. Me. And I sure as heck didn't ask for him.

Two lanky guys enter the station in a panic. The young one is cute and looks about my age. The pair move with the same rhythm, taking long strides, their heads turning right and left. Then they look straight in my direction.

"That's her," the young guy says.

I turn to see if anyone is behind me. No one. I look back. They're smiling.

"Stevie?" the older guy asks. He has some gray sprinkled throughout his brown hair, but he's much younger than I ever pictured my grandfather.

I nod.

"Stevie, I'm Arlo Fulton. I work for your grandfather, Winston Himmel. He asked if we could pick you up." He holds out his hand.

"Oh," I say, accepting the handshake.

"This is my son, Roy."

Roy offers his hand too. He *is* cute, with sandy hair and tanned like a California surfer boy. "Nice to meet you." He's grinning in a way that makes me wonder if he thinks something's funny. "Good to meet you."

I shake his hand but let go quickly. "Hi."

"Sorry we're late," Arlo says. "We actually left early,

but there was an oil spill on the interstate. Traffic was backed up for miles."

Roy looks down at my luggage. "Is this all you have?"

I nod. *All I have.*

They each take a suitcase, and since they're on wheels, I don't object.

We head out of the station and toward the parking lot.

Roy stops. "Dad, you forgot something."

Arlo quits walking. "What?" Then he smacks his forehead and announces, "Kangaroo!"

Chapter Three

Good thing Arlo and Roy are slim, since I'm squeezed between the two of them in the front seat of their truck. It's old, but not as old as the one we had. We called ours Big Momma because of her wide bed. Big Momma smelled of gasoline and oil. Arlo's truck has a pine-scented cardboard tree hanging from the visor. Since it's dangling right in front of me, I get a good whiff of it every time I inhale.

"Winston—" Arlo says, "I mean, your grandfather... he would have picked you up himself, but his quarterly taxes are due."

"Yeah," Roy says, "don't want to mess with the IRS."

My grandfather has never seen me. It seems like he would have set aside time to pick me up. Did he know about me before the accident? I think about the older couple at the bus station. They were excited about seeing their grandkids.

Roy points out the Dallas sights—downtown, the Perot Museum, a round structure atop a skinny building. "That's Reunion Tower. There's a restaurant up there that rotates. I wonder how many people puke out their fancy meals before they get their check."

"They might do it after they get their check," Arlo says. Then he adds, "Sorry, Stevie. Don't mean to be crass. We're just two old bachelors."

"Hey, *you* may be," Roy says. Then he focuses on me. "How old are you, anyway?"

"Thirteen."

"Eighth grade?" Roy asks.

I nod.

"Me too." Roy smiles so big that my neck feels warm.

For a long while, we drive in bumper-to-bumper traffic. But Roy fills the time, telling me about school and which teachers I should avoid. I'm relieved he likes to talk, because then I don't have to. He asks all kinds of questions about living in Taos. And I'm thankful for the ones he doesn't ask.

Traffic eases. The landscape changes to prairie and more sky. If I squint, it sort of reminds me of home. I search for the mountains, but there are only clouds.

Finally, I notice a faded sign with an orange sun on the horizon: TEXAS SUNRISE MOTEL. Then I see the one-level brown building with peeling paint that horseshoes a parking lot with a small pool. No trees, no shrubs, no flowers. Just grass or maybe mowed weeds. VACANCY flashes in neon-red letters.

"Welcome to the Texas Sunrise," Roy says in a strong Texas drawl. "Ain't she purty?"

I'm not sure if he's teasing, so I don't laugh or answer. Because the motel is anything but pretty.

"Town is a half mile west of the motel," Arlo says.

He parks the truck. My gut burns. I'm nervous and dreading what's next.

Arlo and Roy each take a suitcase, and I follow them toward a door posted with THE BLOOMIN' OFFICE in handmade letters.

Roy announces it in an Australian accent: "The Bloomin' Office."

The trill of an adding machine sounds through the door. When Arlo opens it, a bell sounds.

A woman who appears to be about my mom's age glances up from the machine and smiles. An older man with slicked-back white hair and a trim beard stands behind her, staring over her shoulder at the numbers. He reads them aloud.

"Five hundred and forty-seven. Eighty-nine and some odd cents." He sighs.

When the door shuts behind us, he pauses but doesn't glance our way.

"You took longer than I thought," he says, finally looking up.

"Um, well...," I stammer, but then I realize my grandfather is talking to Arlo.

"Oil spill on Thirty-Five," Arlo says, taking a clipboard from the lady.

"Room Seventeen complained about the air conditioner this morning."

Maybe this isn't my grandfather. Maybe this is the manager.

"I'll check on it," says Arlo. He goes to leave but turns back and stares at the old guy, then says to me, "Stevie, it's been a pleasure to meet you. I hope you'll feel at home here."

Roy starts to follow his dad. "See you around the Sunrise. You should get Violet to tell you the story behind the Bloomin' Office."

"I'll save that for you, Roy." Her voice is high-pitched and feathery.

"Yes, ma'am," Roy says, "I'll look forward to it." A bell chimes as the door opens and closes behind them.

I feel awkward, like I don't know where to put my feet.

"I'm Violet," the woman says, smiling. Her hair is pulled back severely with a wide headband. She's kind of pretty with her creamy skin and brown eyes like a deer.

"Good to meet you," I tell her.

The man holds the end of the adding-machine paper, stretching it up as high as his arms can reach.

"Winston," Violet says.

He looks at her and she nudges her head toward me.

This is my grandfather. My parents were right to never tell me about him.

"You look like your father," Winston says.

"That's what everyone says. Except for my eyes."

Winston flinches but looks back down at his paper.

I have my mother's blue eyes. Carmen once told me,

"Your mom and dad don't look alike at all, but you're the spitting image of both of them mixed together."

Winston comes from around the desk and stands there, staring at me awkwardly. "I'll give you a tour."

I'm feeling grumpy. I'm tired and hungry, but I say, "Okay!" so chipper and squeaky, as if he's asked me to go to Disney World. Sometimes I hate myself for acting like everything is okay when it's not. But I'm relieved to know what to do next, even if it's only a short tour.

A Hispanic lady walks into the office just as we're about to leave.

"This is Mercedes," Violet says. "She's the motel housekeeper. *Hola*, Mercedes!" Violet says loudly, like Mercedes is deaf.

"Hello," Mercedes mutters.

"This is Stevie," Violet tells her.

Mercedes nods.

"Hello," I say back. I could have said *hola* and more, because I'd learned quite a lot of Spanish from my neighbors and friends. They liked that I tried. But I have a hunch that won't fly with Mercedes.

Mercedes is younger than Violet, but I can't tell her age. She's petite and curvy. If the boys back home could see her, they'd whistle even if she was wearing her burgundy polyester uniform.

Mercedes tells Winston in a matter-of-fact tone, "You need Ajax and two sheet sets."

"Two sheets sets?" he asks.

"Yes."

"Why?"

"A thief and the other you don't want to know." Her eyes peer sideways at Violet.

"Tell me later," Winston says.

"I have a queasy stomach," Violet explains to me.

Winston uses a key to open a deep drawer. He pulls out an old cigar box, lifts the lid, and takes out two twenty-dollar bills for Mercedes. Then he motions for me to follow him out of the office. He walks fast and speaks without hesitation, like he's done this tour before. "There are thirty rooms, all with two double beds. The bathrooms have a tub/shower combo. There's a coffeemaker with one package of coffee. If they want more, each additional pack costs a buck."

Maybe he's confused and thinks I'm applying for a job. Or maybe he's old and forgetful.

When he doesn't say anything for a long moment, I ask, "Are there microwaves in the rooms?"

I have no idea why I ask that.

He startles. "Ah, no. I've considered it, but our customers would rip us off."

He nods to the swimming pool. It's filled partway with murky green water. "The pool won't open until Memorial Day weekend." There's a sign posted on the back fence with rules. I half expect him to read them to me, but he keeps walking. I'm not a pool person anyway. Give me rivers and lakes. I learned to swim in Eagle Nest Lake and rafted on the Rio Grande.

Then I look back at the pool. Is that where Mom learned to swim? A lump gathers in my throat. I swallow, but it won't budge. I'm glad Winston isn't asking me any questions.

"Violet works the front desk when I'm off. She also keeps the books." We walk back into the office.

Violet has applied a fresh coat of red lipstick since my tour, and she greets us with a big smile. The color makes her look ghostly.

"I'll bet you're hungry," she says.

Winston raises his eyebrows. "Are you?"

"Well, maybe a little."

Winston leads me to another door. When he opens it, I realize I'm in his living quarters. The front room is filled with books—lots of books, stacked all over the table, shelves, and floor. There's a little kitchen area next to the living room. Winston opens the pantry. Three shelves are stocked full with Campbell's soup cans—Cream of Mushroom, Chicken Noodle, Chicken with Rice, and on and on. Once, I saw a bunch of paintings of Campbell's soup cans at the museum. That artist would have loved Winston's pantry.

"Take your pick," he says.

My mother hated processed food. She especially hated Campbell's soup and used to joke about the recipes people made with them. The labels seem to shout out at me. I'm suddenly hungry for Mom's black bean soup. She'd cook it all day with onion and cumin.

"Bean with Bacon," I tell Winston.

He grabs a can and says, "I'll heat it for you while you clean up. You'll be staying in the room to the right."

Chapter Four

THE APARTMENT IS TINY, smaller than the Rockasita—a couple of bedrooms, a kitchenette, and a living area crowded with books, mostly Westerns. The only Western Dad liked was *Lonesome Dove*. He usually read short stories.

Winston says I can have one of the two bathrooms for myself. The Rockasita had only one bathroom. Once when Dad went to Denver for a few days to an heirloom-seed show, Mom and I took turns taking long bubble baths and blaring Billy Joel on the record player. Dad didn't appreciate Joel's talent. That was Mom's nice way of putting it.

I stare at the bedroom, and at my two suitcases. This will be my room. Then I realize if Mom grew up here, this must have been her room too. A chill rushes through my body. I open the dresser drawers. I get on all fours and check under the bed, hoping to see a shred of proof that my mother was here. There're only a few wire hangers in the closet. Nothing else.

"Soup's ready," Winston calls out.

He goes back to work, and I sit at the table, alone with three empty chairs. A mantel clock on top of the bookcase ticks. I lift the spoon to my mouth, but it's hard to swallow. Between bites, I survey the apartment, on the lookout for pictures. But there are none. Every trace of my mother has been swept away from this room, this apartment, *his* life.

I wish I were at the farm. If there was any other place to go, I would flee to it this very minute.

But there is no place.

I finish my soup, wash the bowl and spoon, then head to my new room. Outside the window, the sunset has become a pink sombrero on the rooftop. The motel and vacancy signs reflect on the swimming pool. A breeze travels through my room and flaps the window shade. I try to imagine Mom standing in this very spot. A gust of wind comes without any warning and causes the window to fall and shut on its own. When I discover my own face in the glass, I cup my hands around my eyes. Her eyes. For a long moment, I stand there. Pink sky melts to pale yellow. I slip my finger through the shade's pull and begin to ease it downward. But I stop halfway. *She touched this.*

I fall back onto the bed, hold the pillow over my face, and scream.

Chapter Five

WHEN THE SCHOOL BUS DOOR squeaks open, I wake, gasping. For a moment, I think I'm back in Taos and have over-slept. That never happens. Almost never. Once, I did oversleep. Jorge, the bus driver, had honked and honked the horn. Mom had rushed into my room from the garden.

"Stevie," she'd yelled, "Hop to it!"

Jorge waited.

I got dressed in two minutes flat, beating the world record. By the time I stepped onto the bus, everyone ap-plauded. "Good going, Stevie!" Carmen had hollered from the backseat.

I look out the window and see Roy dashing for the bus. His blond hair looks messy, like he just rolled out of bed himself. He and his dad must live here too. I wonder if he has a girlfriend.

Will Winston enroll me in school today? The thought of meeting a whole bunch of new kids makes my stomach flop, but school will keep my mind busy. Because all I think about now is what I left behind and what left me. Back home, I loved school. Everything but math. Carmen would call me teacher's pet, but she was just teasing. I miss my language arts teacher, Mr. Connor, most. "Words are your tools," he'd say. Some days, we'd walk to the plaza and collect them in our notebooks—*adobe, artist, paint, silver, turquoise, sculpture.* I glance around the room. *Closet, bed, window, empty.* I spot the Australia jar on the corner of the dresser. My mind drifts back to the three of us—Mom, Dad, and me, talking about our plans to go to Australia. Now it will be only me.

The smell of coffee lingers in the kitchen, but the Mr. Coffee is empty and clean. Two newspapers are stacked neatly across from me, the *Dallas Morning News* and the *Fort Worth Star-Telegram.* Winston must have gotten up really early to have already read them and had his coffee. There's a note on the table by the papers. *Pop-Tarts in pantry. Milk in fridge.*

Even breakfast makes me miss home. Most mornings, we ate eggs from our chickens. Collecting eggs was another one of my chores, one I didn't mind doing. I loved our chickens. We had thirteen, a baker's dozen—Rhode Island Reds, Leghorns, and even a Silkie that looked like it was dressed in a white fur coat and hat. We named her after the singer Madonna, because she was such a diva. She pranced around, and if any other chicken got in her space, she went to squawking. Paco said I should sell the chickens for a little extra cash. He said he'd handle it for me. But I gave them to Angelina Cruz instead. She already owned some. I couldn't bear thinking of selling to someone who wanted to raise chickens on a whim. We'd seen so many abandoned ones wandering along the roads. "There goes more coyote bait," Dad used to say.

I toast the Pop-Tarts and eat. There's no dishwasher, so after I finish I fill the sink with hot water and squirt liquid soap under the faucet. I'm not used to a dishwasher anyway. While I rub the sponge against the plate, I search around the room for pictures of Mom or my grandmother. Not one photo. Everything is neat and sterile, as impersonal as a freshly cleaned motel room.

A few minutes later, I slip into the office. Winston is

standing behind the desk. He's with a customer. The man wears a tie with a wrinkled white shirt. I don't remember Winston showing me any irons in the motel rooms.

"How was your stay?" Winston asks, but he doesn't really sound interested in knowing.

"Fine, except—" The man pauses.

He's going to ask about the iron.

"I couldn't get the cable to work."

"There isn't any," says Winston. His tone is matter-of-fact.

"You're kidding? No cable?"

"That's what makes us unique."

The man folds his receipt and tucks it into his pocket. "Cheap," he mutters before opening the door.

"Yes, we are," Winston says.

When the man leaves, I step forward. I want to know about school.

"Morning," my grandfather says without turning to face me.

"Where's Violet?" I ask because I don't feel like saying "good morning."

"She works afternoons."

"I saw Roy leave for school."

He stares down at his ledger.

"Doesn't he go to the middle school?" I ask, even though I know the answer.

"I believe so."

"Shouldn't *I* be in school?" My words come out firm, and I'm kind of proud of myself about that.

He meets my gaze and frowns. "I'll take care of your education needs tomorrow."

My blood boils. I walk outside, wondering if he has a list of obligations with my name at the top.

STEVIE'S NEEDS

1. Roof over head
2. Soup
3. Education

Outside, I settle on a wooden bench. My jaw hurts from me gritting my teeth. Before I arrived, I hardly ever got mad. Traffic zooms pass. *Don't stop here.* I want to tell every car that. *Get the heck as far away as you can from Little Esther, Texas.*

Another person comes out of a room and puts his luggage in the trunk of a car before heading to the office. A moment later, I see Arlo on a ladder, changing a lightbulb outside one of the rooms. He steps down and waves in my direction. I wave back.

Mercedes drives up in an old gold car with a loud muffler. When she stops the engine, her car makes a *put-put-put* sound. "Good morning, Stevie."

"Hi, Mercedes."

She's wearing a chunky beige cardigan over her burgundy uniform. New Mexico mornings are chilly in the spring. It's not that cool outside here, but I guess for Texans it must feel like it is.

"You should go to school. It will make you smart." With that, she walks away, heading toward the laundry room.

The passing cars on the highway hypnotize me.

"Hello."

Startled, I swing around and discover a man and woman in wheelchairs. The man sits upright, his back as straight as a soldier's. His lower legs are missing. The woman's head tilts to the right as if her neck can't handle the weight. Her dark, wispy hair brushes her shoulder.

"Hi," I say.

The woman's head bobs a little, and her mouth

struggles to form the word "Hi-i." I think she may have cerebral palsy, like Betty, one of Mom's friends. Betty's mother used to bring her by the stand every Thursday afternoon. She loved the flowers, and Mom said she'd smell every bouquet before settling on one.

"For a minute, I thought you were the Avon lady," the man says. "But you're just a girl."

I smile. "I guess I am."

"Did you stay here last night?" His long ponytail touches the heart tattoo on his large biceps. The letter *I* is in the center of the heart.

"Did you?" the man asks again.

"I'm sorry"—I look away from his arm, my cheeks warm—"did I what?"

"Did you stay here last night?"

"Yes, I live here now." *Now.* The word feels like a lump in my throat.

"You do?"

I nod.

His eyes squint. "Are you Winston's granddaughter?"

For the first time since arriving, I feel a little encouraged. Maybe Winston was excited about me coming.

Then the man says, "Mercedes told us about meeting you yesterday."

Of course. "I'm Stevie."

"That's a funny name for a girl."

"I guess it is." I don't bother explaining the Fleetwood Mac connection.

"The only girl I've heard of with that name is Stevie Nicks."

"My parents were fans."

"Sorry, can't say the same." He stretches his arm toward me and we shake. His grasp is firm, and I have to resist rubbing my knuckles when he lets go.

"I'm Horace. And this is my wife, Ida."

The *I* in the heart.

Ida smiles at me, and her fingers smooth her hair.

"Nice to meet you." I move closer to her and hold out my hand. She grabs my fingertips and squeezes.

"Until yesterday, I didn't know Winston had any children, much less a granddaughter. Of course, he's a private man. No crime in that."

"Do you and Ida stay here a lot?"

"For the last eight years," Horace says. "We moved

right after we got married. Still haven't gone on our Pensacola honeymoon, have we, Ida?"

Ida makes a little sound that I think is a sort of laugh.

"But we will," Horace says. "I can promise you that. Today I'm just wanting to know where that Avon lady is. She's supposed to bring Ida her Sweet Honesty cologne. Have you ever smelled it?"

"No. Sorry."

"Smells sweet as Ida. If that lady would just get here. We've been waiting two days for her."

And even though it's only seven fifty in the morning, I find myself looking out to the highway in search of her too.

Chapter Six

I'VE TURNED MY ROOM upside down trying to find anything that my mother left behind. I want to know her secret life. The life before me. I raise the mattress, hoping to discover a diary. Instead a tiny spider scampers out, escaping to the floor.

Whenever I went to Carmen's house to spend the night, I'd get homesick. It didn't help that Carmen and the other girls liked to do séances. Someone would want to bring back their crazy aunt, and Carmen would turn out the lights and gather us in a circle. A tree branch would scratch against the window, causing us all to scream. It never failed to happen. Later, when everyone else was asleep, I'd close my eyes and remember a favorite dream. And that's exactly what I do now. I'm at the ocean.

There's laughing, music, and waves. I must be a toddler, because Mom's holding my hands, leading me to the water's edge. The ocean's foam kisses my chubby knees.

I've remembered bits of the dream through the years. I see a bonfire on the beach. My mom is there, and a man playing a guitar, singing. Even though the man doesn't look like my dad, I know it is him. It must be him. People sometimes look different in dreams. In this one, he has a head of curly hair. It's a good dream, because every time I think about it I feel warm all over.

Since I'm not going to school today, I decide to walk around with Mom's camera. She'd just traded in her old one that needed film for this digital one. Dad and I had tried to convince her for years to switch, but she was stubborn about taking photos the old-fashioned way. I can take a hundred pictures if I want. The land surrounding the motel is flat and bare. I focus on the Texas Sunrise Motel sign and take a long shot. Then I move in closer and concentrate on the base, where a patch of short stems poke through the weeds. The leaves look familiar, but I can't remember what they remind me of. A cloud of pink blooms enters my thoughts. "Phlox!" I say it so loud and glance around to see if anyone heard me, but I'm alone. It's quiet except for the highway traffic whizzing by.

We had phlox all around the Rockasita. The memory of it makes my heart leap. The blooms aren't here yet, but I focus the lens and *click, click, click.*

Back home, flowers meant work. I had my share of the chores—watering, pulling weeds, turning the compost pile. But now, as I look around the motel grounds, I can't help thinking how much better even a dump like this would look with some flowers and green. For a minute, my head is like a lighthouse, turning right and left, then back right again, searching for the perfect place for a garden. But planting a garden would mean I'd be putting down roots. And I'm getting out of here as soon as I'm old enough, to return to the farm.

A UPS truck turns into our parking lot as I make my way back. The driver hops out with a box, goes inside the office, and returns to the truck. She waves to me as she drives off. I open the door, wishing there was a way to get into the apartment without going through the Bloomin' Office.

"You have a package," Winston says, tapping his pen on the box.

The record player, records, and photo albums have arrived.

Chapter Seven

IT'S MY THIRD DAY HERE, and Winston still hasn't said when he's going to enroll me in school. He hasn't mentioned my parents, either. Doesn't it matter to him that Mom isn't here anymore? My eyes do the blur-and-burn thing again. They did that when my other stuff arrived too. That's why the box is still under my bed.

Since the sun is up, I change so that I'm ready in case Winston decides to take care of my "education needs" today. At seven thirty, Roy walks from his apartment toward the road. I open the window and softly call out his name.

He stops, glances about, then keeps walking.

I say it a bit louder. "Roy!"

He spins around. When he sees me, he smiles and

hurries over to my window. He's all legs and arms, and he moves like a whirligig gathering speed.

"Playing hooky again?"

I shrug.

"Winston will probably enroll you today. Remember what I told you—don't take Spanish. The teacher piles on the homework."

I don't tell him that I already know a good bit of Spanish and that I'll probably take it as my elective. Everyone needs an easy A.

"Do you want to hear the Bloomin' Office story?" he asks.

"Sure."

Roy checks his watch. "I'll make it quick. We had a few Aussies staying here a couple of years ago. They were doing a road trip around Texas. They started drinking in the mornings and didn't quit until after midnight. Come checkout day, they were so drunk that they circled the motel, walking laps around the parking lot. We couldn't figure out what the heck they were doing. One of them asked Dad, 'Where's the bloomin' office?'"

"That's funny."

"Yeah, it was. After they left, we all had a good laugh about it. Dad made the sign."

We hear the roar of an engine, and then the bus turns into the parking lot.

"Better go!" he says. "See you in school! Remember: don't take Spanish!"

"I've already forgotten," I tell him.

Roy sprints toward the bus, his backpack dangling from his arm. He probably has a girlfriend.

I make my way to the kitchen, where Winston is fixing a fresh pot of coffee. He must live on the stuff. I toast two blueberry Pop-Tarts for breakfast. In less than forty-eight hours, I've managed to destroy all the healthy eating habits Mom enforced my entire life. We raised practically everything we ate.

"Do you want some coffee?" Winston asks.

"No," I snap. "Never touch the stuff." I'm hoping to get a reaction out of him, but it doesn't work. He hardly looks in my eyes when he speaks, and the few times he has, he quickly fixed his gaze on some nearby item.

"I called your teacher, Beatrice Crump. She said today would be good as any to begin."

"Do you mean my homeroom teacher?"

Winston sighs. My questions seem to cause him to do that, as if to answer takes a lot of energy. "Well," he says, "the class is in her home, so I guess you could call her a homeroom teacher."

"I'm not going to the middle school?"

He stares at me a long minute before speaking. "When I agreed to take you in, I made a commitment to raise you. And I will raise you as I see fit."

My face burns. I reach for the coffeepot and pour myself a cup. The liquid is strong and hot. I swish it around in my mouth, burning my tongue before swallowing. Black coffee is bitter. Like my new life. The image of me catching the bus with Roy each morning and making friends with the other kids on his school bus evaporates.

Dad would call Winston's van a gas guzzler. Although Dad's old truck wasn't much better. He always blamed his frequent trips to the gas station on the mountain climb. We drive toward town, and for that I'm grateful. I long to see something besides highway. I loved our farm, but I also loved the plaza. We went there a lot for all kinds of events—music, art shows, or just sitting on a bench and people-watching. There were all kinds of crazy tourists. The tourists probably came there to watch *us*.

Soon we begin to approach houses that look as if they were built at the turn of the last century, large and lovely with wide porches and gingerbread trim, like pretty, plump women dressed in lace. I can see the square, but before we reach it, Winston parks in front of a grand Victorian house. It's a pale-blue two-story. A Southern magnolia tree in the front yard towers above the roofline. The lawn is mowed, but the roses and shrubs are overgrown. The flower beds next to the house are crowded with weeds and grass.

"This is it," Winston says.

We climb the steps that stretch across the entire front porch. Winston rings the doorbell. No one answers. We wait for what seems long enough to boil water. I'm beginning to wonder why Winston doesn't try again when he presses the buzzer and knocks loudly.

Another long minute passes before we hear someone unlatching a lock. Then another. And another. The door creaks open.

An old woman—a very old woman—with a badly dyed black pixie haircut and bright cherry lipstick stands before us. Her tiny body seems to be held up by a cane with a leopard-print handle. Even so, she quakes from the effort. She raises her chin, peering through her green-framed glasses, and smiles at me. Then she turns her attention to Winston.

"Winston Himmel, haven't seen you in a dozen years." She says it like she's not expecting us.

Winston rubs at his beard. "Has it been that long? It can't be."

"At least. I ran into you at the convenience store. We waved at each other between the pickled eggs and beef jerky. No, sir, haven't seen you up close since right after Daisy's last class."

My heart skips a beat. Was this old lady my mother's teacher?

Winston nods fast as she speaks. His face turns white as sand and he holds up a hand to stop her. "Um, yes, I guess it has been that long. Well, this is your pupil."

She looks up at me. "Hello, young lady. I'm Mrs. Crump."

"Hi, I'm Stevie."

She touches my wrist with her icy hands. "We're going to have an exciting journey together."

How could this old lady take me anywhere exciting? I wonder what Roy is doing at the middle school, what my friends at my old school are doing, what Mr. Connor is saying. Something exciting, probably.

"Three o'clock?" Winston asks.

"Seems you do remember some things," Mrs. Crump says.

As Winston turns to leave, Mrs. Crump tells me, "I'm so sorry about your mother and father."

When she says that, Winston's back tenses. He walks away and is gone. It may have bothered him to hear those words, but I've needed to hear them. I didn't realize how much until then.

"Thank you," I say.

Mrs. Crump motions me inside and toward the mahogany staircase with a worn runner hugging the steps. "Shall we? We'll need to get to the second floor."

I wonder how she will make it up, but she lowers her body onto a compact box seat attached to the side of the staircase. She pushes a button and the chairlift moves her up, up, up.

I stand at the bottom watching until she reaches the top. I'm still watching when she gets out and stands.

"Do you need a ride?" she asks. "I can send my chair-lift to you."

My face feels hot. I didn't mean to stare. It's a bad habit of mine.

"No, I'm sorry. I just never saw—"

"You'll need to try it sometime." Both hands rest firmly on her cane in front of her like she's a dancer on a chorus line. I picture a top hat on her head. A giant bee hangs from the ceiling, not a real one, but one that looks like it's made from papier-mâché. I start my climb. Some of them squeak.

"Best thing invented since sliced bread," she says.

"The bee?"

"The bee?" She looks up. "Oh, the bee. The bee was made by my other student. She gave it to me. I thought it was stunning. That bee is a reminder to me of what can happen when you let students do what they want. They learn anyway. She designed and made it herself.

"But I was talking about my chairlift. The neighbors who are my age haven't seen their second floors in decades. They could have an entire family of squatters living up-stairs for all they know. Too much of my life is up here. My books, my journals. And I adore looking at town through the north window. Life's hurdles are for jumping."

She is jabbering away, but when she takes a breath I ask, "You have another student?"

"Yes, Flora. She's about your age. She's not here today. You'll meet her soon enough."

I'm happy there will be someone else. Someone my age. Coming here won't feel as strange now. Maybe we'll end up being good friends. I miss Carmen. I miss all my friends. Carmen didn't even say good-bye, but I kind of knew she wouldn't. She hates mush. When we'd go to the movies, she always went to the bathroom during the sad parts. She didn't go to my parents' funeral either. She said she was sick. Some people would have been mad if their best friend wasn't there, but I understand Carmen. When she heard about my parents, she said, "That really sucks!" and I knew she meant it. I saw her eyes tear up before she looked away. She loved my parents. They were a lot better than hers. Every week, her parents went to a casino in Santa Fe and lost most of their paychecks. And in her way, she did say good-bye. The last time I saw her was right after Paco checked me out of school. She walked over to us, and Paco said, "Take your time. I'll meet you in the car." As soon as he said that, Carmen had a look of panic in her eyes. Then she lifted her chin, punched my shoulder, and said, "Don't be so perfect. Skip school sometimes." She turned and walked toward the bus.

"Hey," I called back to her.

She stopped and faced me.

"Try going to class sometime. You might learn a thing or two."

We laughed and she walked backward for a while, smiling at me. Then she dashed toward the bus. That was only a couple of weeks ago. It seems more like a year.

On the second level, I follow Mrs. Crump as she inches across the wood floor, her cane *tap tap*ping as she steps. She moves at a turtle's pace. I shuffle my feet slowly so I don't run into her. When she notices, she pauses and points to a large library table that stretches the length of the room. "I'll meet you over there."

I settle in a seat across from a thick atlas and wait. The table is shiny and smells of orange oil. Mrs. Crump is at the halfway point. To keep from staring, I thumb through the pages of the atlas. There are tons of maps, and I get lost looking at the detailed one of Australia. I feel like a rock landed in the pit of my stomach.

When Mrs. Crump reaches the table, I get up and rush to her side.

"Let me get your chair."

"Daisy did a good job teaching you manners."

After I return to my spot, she studies me. "My, oh my, you have your mother's eyes, blue as the Mediterranean Sea."

"Thank you."

"So if I call you Daisy, forgive me."

Three times. She's said my mother's name three times. I like Mrs. Crump.

Mrs. Crump decides today should be about getting acquainted. "Why don't you write an essay about your journey here?"

"The bus ride?"

"If that's how you arrived."

While I think back to the trip across Texas, Mrs. Crump pulls books from the shelves behind her. I offer to help, but she says she can manage. It's painful to watch her struggle with the task, but she insists, so I don't try to help. She chooses a short-story collection, an algebra book, and a poetry anthology.

I begin to write. I write about saying good-bye to my neighbors and Carmen, and shutting the front door of the Rockasita. I write about the long bus ride across Texas and seeing tumbleweeds. I write about the lady knitting the red scarf for her nephew. I dig in my purse and pull out the candy wrapper where I scribbled, *Everyone always stops for a giant on a unicycle.* I'm writing about the kids on the bus when I hear twelve chimes coming from the Methodist church across the street.

"Stevie, you must be a writer," she says. "Words seem to flow from your pen."

I shrug, but I wish it was true.

"Let's take a break for lunch downstairs in the dining room."

"I forgot to bring something." Really I'm ticked that Winston didn't think of it.

"Don't worry," Mrs. Crump says. "There's a great big pot of soup on my stove."

Before taking the stairs, I try to help her into her chairlift, but she pulls back. "Stevie, you and I are going to be together a lot, but you won't be around me twenty-four hours a day. I need to do things on my own. I can't get used to anyone helping me. I have to stay independent. Understand?" Her tone is firm.

"Yes." Then I add, "Ma'am," remembering Roy. I want to fit in.

Mrs. Crump eases into her chairlift, rear first, then her legs. When she settles there, she tells me, "Now wait here just one moment."

Down, down, down she goes. After she gets out, she pushes the button and sends it up to the second floor. "Give it a go."

And I do. The chairlift moves slow and steady. I slide by the ceiling of the first floor, and when I catch sight of my reflection in a huge mirror hung in the hallway, I crack up. I look up at the bee and laugh harder. It's as if I'm releasing some of the bad stuff that's happened, letting it seep out a little as I travel down the staircase in Mrs. Crump's chairlift.

She waits for me at the bottom of the stairs. "See? I told you it was jolly fun."

A spicy aroma fills the air. My stomach growls. Mrs. Crump tells me to sit at the dining room table and that she will bring my bowl to me. A drawer squeaks open and there's clanking. Then I hear a crash and something shattering.

Mrs. Crump curses loudly.

I scoot my heavy dining chair away from the table just as she calls out to me. "Don't get up, dear. I have a cleaning lady coming later. She'll get it."

The dining room walls are covered in gold wallpaper that has started to peel away. A portrait of George Washington stares at me. A moment later, Mrs. Crump walks into the dining room with her cane in one hand and my bowl of soup in the other. She's smiling and seems to be unaware of her hand quivering and soup splashing out of the bowl and onto the floor. I get up to rescue my lunch.

"Thank you!" I say, easing the bowl from her hands.

The soup, minestrone with lots of vegetables, is lukewarm but good—homemade, not oversalted like Winston's Campbell's collection.

When she joins me, she asks all kinds of questions about the motel and the people who live there.

I want to ask about Mom but don't. It's probably best to bring that subject up a little at a time, kind of like savoring a chocolate Easter bunny for an entire week.

But I think of the questions I'll ask. How long was Mom her student? What was her favorite subject? And what I want to know more than anything: did she get along with my grandfather?

After lunch, we make our way upstairs. Mrs. Crump rides, but this time I walk. I continue to write about my journey to Little Esther. For a long time, the words come. About a half hour later, my hands ache and I drop my pen to stretch my fingers. Across the table, Mrs. Crump's eyes are closed and her head rests on her left shoulder. I watch for her chest to rise, but it's perfectly still.

"Mrs. Crump?" I whisper. Then a little louder I say, "Mrs. Crump?"

My heart pounds in my ears. I rush to Mrs. Crump's side, but I lack the courage to touch her. My body twists from side to side, but my feet are concrete. I slowly stretch my arm toward her.

Just before I reach her wrist, I hear a flat whistling. *Zzzz, zzzz.* Mrs. Crump's shoulders crouch forward a little, but then they move back into place, like she is fighting sleep. I'm so relieved, I return to my seat, pick up my pen, and go back to writing.

When the church bell chimes two times, Mrs. Crump

awakens and says, "If you like, you can finish your essay for homework. I think we'd better move on to geography."

She opens the atlas. "Any place in particular that you'd prefer to study?"

Without hesitation, I tell her, "Australia."

Chapter Eight

ON THE WAY BACK to the motel, I'm quiet and Winston is too. I close my eyes and see Dad and me scuba diving near the Great Barrier Reef. We'd find pieces of coral, and back onshore Mom would take pictures of our treasures. If only it had really happened.

Roy must be trying to break a world record for fastest lawn-mowing guy. Even at his quick speed, his rows of clipped, dry grass are perfectly even.

After Winston goes to the office, I go over to Roy. He stops the lawn mower when he sees me walking toward him.

"Played hooky again, huh?" A bead of sweat trickles down his cheek.

"I went to school today."

"You did? How'd I miss you?"

He doesn't give me a chance to answer. "Are you in honors classes? Hey, you didn't register for that Spanish class, did you?"

"Well, that's because I wasn't at your school." I'm feeling like a freak, the girl who eats Pop-Tarts and soup and rides in an old lady's chairlift.

"Are you at the private school?" Roy asks. "If so, I need to inform you their football team stinks."

"My school doesn't have a football team."

We're interrupted by a UPS truck that has turned into the parking lot. Seeing it reminds me of the record player. I still haven't unpacked it. The driver waves and we wave back.

Roy rests his forearms on the lawn mower handle. "Are we doing riddles? Because I'm not good at those."

For a second, I'm caught up in how cute his forehead is when he wrinkles it. Then I end the mystery. "Winston took me to a tutor. Beatrice Crump."

Roy slowly grins. "Old Lady Crump?"

"You know her?"

"Not personally, but she's famous around here."

"Why?"

"She used to teach elementary school—sixth grade, I think. She left before I got there. I heard they made her retire because she had epilepsy."

"Mrs. Crump has seizures?" I really need to find out where she keeps her phone.

"Nope, she falls asleep all the time. Even in the middle of sentences."

"Do you mean narcolepsy?"

"Yep, Sherlock, she falls asleep at the drop of a hat."

"I think she's wonderful—I mean, for someone her age."

"What's that? A hundred and four?"

I hardly know Mrs. Crump, but for some reason I feel protective toward her. I don't tell Roy how I thought she was dead, how she didn't wake up until the church across the street sounded its bell at two o'clock. "So you mow the grass at the motel?"

"More like weed mowing."

I grab the base of a dandelion, and the soft ground allows me to pluck it up easily, including the taproot.

I wave it under his nose. "Did you know you can eat dandelion greens?"

Roy pulls away. "You mean *you* can eat dandelion greens. Is that the kind of food you eat in New Mexico?"

I roll my eyes. "They're very nutritious, but they're an acquired taste." Something I'd never acquired. I almost shudder remembering Mom trying to persuade me to sip her green juice concoction. When I refused, she'd say, "I'm going to live to be a hundred." She might as well have eaten potato chips and fried food for three meals a day.

"You gotta have a football team to root for," Roy says. "Guess you'll have to go to the Panthers games with me next year."

The UPS truck leaves the parking lot, and Roy starts up the lawn mower again. I walk away, dreaming about sitting in the bleachers with him, cheering for every touchdown scored by the Little Esther Panthers.

Chapter Nine

WINSTON LETS ME OUT in front of Mrs. Crump's house for my second day of class. "See you at three."

I'm about to say thanks, but I'm caught off guard by a girl banging on the front door with her fist. "Come on! I've gotta pee!"

I glance back, expecting to see Winston making his way down the street, but he's sitting out there in the driveway watching, and I guess waiting for Mrs. Crump to answer. You never know. She may have died in her sleep.

"Are you Flora?" I ask the girl.

She turns around. She has big dark eyes and black hair with one thick white streak. It looks like it's been dipped in paint, but I think it's natural.

"Frida," she snaps.

I'm confused.

The door opens. "Good morning, girls," Mrs. Crump says.

She waves to Winston, who lifts his hand up for a second before backing out onto the road.

"Flora, it looks like you've met Stevie."

"Frida." Then she spells her name. "F-r-i-d-a."

"Of course," Mrs. Crump says. "Forgive me."

"That's what you said the last hundred times," Frida mutters. She stomps up the stairs.

By the time Mrs. Crump and I are on the second floor, Frida is nowhere in sight. Then I remember. She needed to go to the bathroom.

MRS. CRUMP GIVES EACH OF US an old, dusty English textbook and asks us to turn to a short story, "The Lottery."

"Would you mind reading it aloud, Stevie?"

I hate when a teacher asks me to do that. At Christmas, my parents would watch me as I opened each gift. I couldn't stand that. It felt like I was under a spotlight. Reading in front of classmates felt the same way.

"Would you?" she repeats.

Frida smirks.

"Okay," I say.

While I read, Frida doodles in her notebook, and when I finish, Mrs. Crump says, "Oh, that was nice. You read beautifully."

Frida snorts. "Yeah, beauty-full-lee."

I look at her doodle. Either she's playing hangman by herself or she's a little obsessed with nooses.

So much for us being good friends.

At lunch, Frida picks her peanut butter sandwich into tiny pieces and makes a hill in the middle of her napkin. When she catches me watching her, she mouths, *Boo!*

I'm not used to anyone like her. Carmen was a little rebellious, but she wasn't mean. Even the teachers loved her and forgave her whenever she skipped school.

Mrs. Crump tells us to work on our geography reports. "Frida, what are you going to be writing about?"

"Pluto," she says.

Mrs. Crump smiles. "That should be fascinating."

I wonder if she heard Frida. I start reading about Australia's export products. Mrs. Crump drifts off to sleep. Frida glares at me as she eases back her chair and gets up. She doesn't say a word, just heads down the stairs and out the front door.

Chapter Ten

ROY TELLS ME Frida was kicked out of school for skipping.

"Kicked out?"

"Well, suspended," he explains. "Did you see her mom?"

I did, and I know what he's getting at, but I just kind of nod. Frida's mom rides a motorcycle, and today she wore a black leather vest and pants. When we came out of the house, she was talking on her cell phone. Not once did she look or speak to Frida. Not even after she hung up. Frida looked at me like she was daring me to say something. I hollered, "See you tomorrow."

She rolled her eyes, then pulled on her helmet and climbed onto the back of her mom's motorcycle. They took off, with her mom's thick braid dancing in the wind.

"Her mom is in a motorcycle gang," Roy says.

"A gang? You mean like the Hell's Angels?"

"Something like that," Roy says. "They hang out at the diner all morning on Saturdays. I don't think they break the law or anything. But they're a scary-looking bunch."

"I try not to judge people by how they look." I wonder what Roy would have thought of Dad's tattoos?

"Well, excuse me for judging," Roy says. Then his wink causes me to look away.

AT DINNER, Winston asks me about Frida. "Who was that girl this morning?"

"The one at Mrs. Crump's door?"

"Yes, the one who had a bee in her bonnet to get inside." He slurps a spoonful of tomato soup.

"Frida. She's Mrs. Crump's other student."

"Frida who?"

"I think her last name is James." I remember seeing it on her notebook.

"She's a James?"

"Well, a Frida James."

"Stay away from her," he says.

And just the way he says that makes me want to be her new best friend.

"What'd she do?" I ask.

"I don't know Frida, but her mom gets this town in an uproar with all of her motorcycle friends."

"What's wrong with riding a motorcycle?"

Winston grimaces. "Nothing's wrong with motorcycles. I had one for a while."

"You did?" My dad had an old Harley, but he never got it fixed. So he never rode it. He always acted funny when I said, "When are you going to fix it so you can take me for a ride?" One time, he snapped when I asked. "Enough with the motorcycle. That takes money."

Winston drums his fingers on the table. It's weird the way he does it. Not like most people who are impatient, tapping their fingers quickly. His fingers seem to dance to a tune, like someone playing the piano.

TONIGHT I LIE IN BED and stare at the Australia jar. I wonder how much money is in there, but I don't dare count it. I'm afraid the amount will depress me. Then I remember the book Mrs. Crump lent me. I pull it from my backpack and crawl into bed with it. There aren't as many pictures as I'd like, but the words take me there.

There's a little island off the south coast of Australia called Kangaroo Island. Koalas, penguins, sea lions, and of course kangaroos live there. Rugged cliffs overlook isolated beaches, and beyond that, land stretches across the hills. Visitors can rent out the lighthouse-keeper's cottage at Cape Willoughby on Dudley Peninsula.

I WAKE UP with the book on the bed next to me. The clock says it's seven thirty. I get out of bed and dress in a hurry. Then I realize two things: it's Saturday and I'm hungry. There's a seashell in the kitchen window that I never noticed until now. It makes me think of the dream I always have about being a little kid at the beach. I can see Mom holding up a seashell, just like that one, to my ear. "Hear the ocean?" she says.

All at once, I remember the dream I had last night of Kangaroo Island. In my dream, I opened the door to the lighthouse-keeper's cottage and Mom and Dad walked out, hand in hand. We spent the day on a little farm with goats. I kept thinking here we are in Australia with goats when we should be looking at the kangaroos and koalas. It didn't matter, though. We were together. I awoke in the middle of it.

I hope I have that dream again.

Winston is at his desk in the office with a mug of coffee and the *Dallas Morning News*.

"Can you help Violet clean the rooms this morning?" he asks. Before I can answer, he adds, "Mercedes didn't come to work today."

"Is she sick?"

"No, she's celebrating some saint's birthday. She celebrates all of them." Winston says it like he's not so sure that's what she's doing.

I can't seem to wipe away the image of a huge birthday cake with a saint dressed in a long brown robe made of chocolate icing on top.

"Violet will show you what to do."

I quickly change into my grubby jeans and Dad's Rolling Stones T-shirt. I brought all of his T-shirts—Pink Floyd, Van Halen, and Led Zep. They're baggy on me, but they're soft, and they still smell like the Gain laundry soap we used.

I gobble down a strawberry Pop-Tart. I hate to admit it, but Pop-Tarts are the best thing I was never allowed to eat.

Violet isn't dressed shabby at all. She's wearing one of her floral dresses that I've silently started to name. This one is Party Pink—peonies the size of salad plates cover the entire dress. Her headband matches perfectly.

"Do you need an old T-shirt?" I ask her.

"No, thank you. I brought an apron."

When Violet ties the rickrack-trimmed apron around her waist, she reminds me of those 1950s sitcom moms I've seen on the TV Land channel.

She fetches a clipboard from the office with the list of rooms to clean. We pass by Room 12, where a bunch of boxes inside the room block the window.

"Is somebody living there?"

Violet shakes her head. "No, we don't book that room." She doesn't offer anything more. Together we walk to the laundry room, where the linen closet is. As we near it, we hear a loud racket—*punch ker rack, punch ker rack, punch ker rack.*

"Spin cycle," Violet says, pulling Mercedes's cleaning cart from the room. Then she slips her hand into her apron pocket and pulls out two pairs of yellow Playtex gloves. She offers me one pair.

Putting her gloves on over her rosy press-on nails takes a long time. While she does that, I try to imagine her as a child. Violet becomes a small version of herself wearing black patent Mary Jane shoes instead of white pumps. She's in class, sharpening her pencils and tucking them in a pink plastic case. The teacher asks a question and she stretches her hand up toward the ceiling.

"Yoo-hoo?" Violet is waving her hand in front of my face.

I snap out of my daydream. "Sorry."

"I'll clean the bathrooms," she tells me. "Winston is particular when it comes to toilets and tubs. He wants them spic and span. Why don't you strip the beds, dust, and vacuum?"

One of the beds is still made. Obviously no one has slept there, but Violet says we need to change it anyway.

"A Winston rule," she explains.

It's interesting how Winston is picky about clean rooms but it doesn't seem like he has painted or updated the motel since the last century.

At the foot of the bed, I find a white lacy nightgown. When I pick it up, Violet snatches it out of my hand. "I'll take that to the Lost and Found Department."

"We have a Lost and Found Department?"

"Of course," she says seriously. "People leave things all the time, especially phone chargers."

After pulling the pillowcases off the pillows, I toss them into the dirty-laundry cart. Then I search for a dusting cloth and furniture polish. I find the cloth but no spray. When I go into the bathroom to see if Violet has it, I catch her holding the gown up and studying her reflection in the mirror. She tilts her head to one side and then the other.

Just seeing her with that nightgown makes me feel a little sad. I don't know why. If it had been a cool top, I might have done the same thing.

She notices me standing there, staring at her, but she doesn't seem embarrassed. She just shrugs and says, "I would have picked pink."

I dump the coffee grounds from the filter holder and start to leave two packages of coffee instead of one, just to be a little rebellious.

Violet stops me. "Another Winston rule."

Seems the only things I know about my grandfather are his rules.

After Violet and I finish, she heads straight for her car. She forgot and took the nightgown with her. Back at the office, Winston surprises me when he says, "Thank you for helping Violet clean the rooms this morning."

"Did my mother ever clean the motel rooms?"

Winston clears his throat. "It was her weekend job when she was a teenager."

I wait, hoping he'll say more about Mom, but he pulls the pages of his newspaper together and folds them. That ticks me off. Why can't he say anything about her? Why hasn't he even said he was sorry the accident happened? Or how he wishes she was still alive. I think about asking Winston all those questions, but instead I say, "I didn't know we had a Lost and Found Department." I'm a big chicken.

Winston's eyebrows knit together. Then he bends over and disappears behind the desk. When he straightens, he plops a Stetson hatbox in front of me. A handmade label is taped across the lid: LOST AND FOUND DEPARTMENT.

Back in the room, I pull the record player out of the box, but I can't bring myself to plug it in.

Chapter Eleven

A WEEK HAS PASSED since I cleaned the rooms with Violet. Mercedes is back to work. Most mornings now, I'm up early enough to see her arrive. I glance at my watch often and subtract an hour, wondering what my friends are doing at that very minute. It's six in the morning. That means five a.m. in Taos. No doubt where they are. In bed.

The sun is still low in the sky here. Even Roy is awake. From my window, I see him loading tackle boxes into a truck bed. I dress quickly, putting on yesterday's T-shirt and jeans from the pile on the floor.

Outside, Roy tells me, "We're going fishing at the lake."

"There's a lake nearby?"

"You need to get out more. It's Lake Little Esther. We go most Saturdays this time of year, but we usually leave before dawn. Last night, we stayed up late watching horror movies."

"Better you than me." I hate scary movies.

"Fishing?"

"I couldn't kill a fish."

Roy smirks. "So I'm a fish murderer?"

"That's another name for it." I manage to sound serious.

"Sorry," he says, and he really seems like he is. "I just like spending time with my dad."

I feel like he punched me in the gut, and I guess it shows.

He quickly says, "Sorry. I mean—"

"I was just kidding. There's nothing wrong with fishing."

He looks so relieved. "You got me. I guess I thought you were one of those hippy vegetarians. We don't have many of those in Texas."

"There are a few carnivores outside cowboy country. I love hamburgers."

Roy slowly grins, and for the first time I notice he

has a dimple on the right cheek. "Did you get dressed in a hurry?"

One dimple. Could he be any cuter?

"Well?" He's waiting. Did he ask me something?

"What?"

He points to my T-shirt. "Is that the new style?"

I look down. ROLLING STONES is spelled backward. My T-shirt is inside out. I feel my face heat up like a furnace.

Roy rubs his chin and tilts his head, sizing me up. "I like it. I'm going to start wearing mine that way."

His teasing makes me feel a little better, but I'm still thinking about what he said earlier, how he likes to spend time with his dad. Once, I went fishing with Dad at Red River. He'd been bugging me about going with him for the last couple of years. One day I gave in. I hated it—the wiggly worms, the stink on my hands, the poor fish flopping with the hook attached to its guts. I never went back.

If Dad were alive, I'd fish every day of my life with him.

Arlo comes out with the ice chest. "Morning, Stevie."

"Morning."

"Ready, buddy?" Arlo asks Roy.

I head back to the apartment. Mercedes is pushing the cart to her first room. She waves at me and I wave back. Another long Saturday at the Texas Sunrise Motel.

ON MONDAY, Mrs. Crump suggests we write poems. Her earrings have orange balls hanging from thin chains that swing when she moves her head. Frida told her they were awesome. I couldn't tell if she really liked them or not.

I used to think I hated poetry, until Mr. Connor read "Aimless Love" by Billy Collins to our class. And then, just like the poet's love for the wren and the mouse and the bar of soap, I fell hard for poetry. I filled an entire notebook with poems I wrote and read. But I didn't pack it. I gave it to the trash can instead.

Frida is chewing on her pencil. She looks bored, glancing around the room like she's planning her next escape. But a moment later, she works up her pen into a mad speed. I'm impressed, until I notice she's writing *This Stinks* over and over again.

Five minutes later, Mrs. Crump asks, "Do you want a few prompts?"

I nod.

Mrs. Crump tears a sheet of paper from a notebook and writes. Her hand trembles a little. I wonder how long it took her to put in those earrings. Then she turns the page to face me. "Here are three prompts to get your creative juices going."

The Highway
Last Night's Dinner
Mother

When I read the last prompt, I forget how to breathe. I focus on the other two. *The highway.* Since I've already written about the trip to my grandfather's home, I reject that one right off. *Last night's dinner.* After a long think, I can only come up with Campbell's Cheddar Cheese soup, Ritz crackers, and my grandfather's quiet demeanor. It's off to a dull start.

Frida is on her second page. Mrs. Crump is asleep. I stare at the remaining prompt—*Mother.* The letters blur in front of me. My head is full of images. Mom teaching me to dance the twist, singing her favorite songs, teasing my dad. Something snaps in me and I can't hold it back. I rest my head on the table and try to hide behind my arm, but it's no use. I break down like a river rushing over a dam.

Frida nudges me with a tissue box.

I take one.

She pulls two more out and hands them to me. Then she goes back to her list as if nothing happened.

Poetry.

Chapter Twelve

HORACE WANTS TO KNOW when the pool will open.

"Memorial Day weekend," Winston says. "Always Memorial Day weekend." He doesn't even look at Horace, just keeps stapling papers.

"I know, but do you consider that Friday or Saturday?" Horace asks.

"The weekend is Saturday and Sunday." Winston's voice is matter-of-fact.

Horace moves his wheelchair back and forth an inch or two, reminding me of someone shifting their weight on their feet. "Well, some folks think of Friday, at least Friday night, as the weekend."

Now Winston looks up. "Some folks want to celebrate too much."

I'm wondering if Winston is talking about Mercedes. It's another saint's birthday and she took off to celebrate with her family. Since it's Saturday, that means I'm cleaning rooms with Violet. I don't mind, because now when I dust, I think of my mother dusting the same spots. When I vacuum, I remember her vacuuming and singing like she did at home. She'd belt out her favorite part to that Elton John song, *Hold me closer, tiny dancer,* her voice rising over the loud hum of the vacuum. Mom's face showed such emotion, I could almost see the spotlight on her, and an audience watching her every move. As soon as she turned the vacuum off, she'd go back to being Mom.

When we finish cleaning the first room, I ask Violet, "Does Horace swim?"

"What?" Violet is wearing her Triple P outfit—purple, posies, and polka dots. The gold-fringe scarf left behind in one of the rooms last week is tied around her neck. I wonder if she ever took it to the Lost and Found Department. And how about the nightgown we found the first time I helped her clean?

"Horace asked when the pool would open," I tell her. "Does he swim?"

"He and Ida like to sit by the pool. They enjoy watching people swim." She says this like it makes sense to her. And it kind of does to me too, now.

Maybe they're pretending they're in Pensacola, on the honeymoon they've never taken. It's like when I daydream about my mother being young, doing the same things I'm doing now.

Cleaning the rooms doesn't take long, because there are never more than six or seven booked each night. Winston would have more if he fixed up the place. He could even make it hip, turn it retro. But one glance around proves it's already retro—the pale bookcase headboard and matching dresser, the metal armchair, the avocado drapes. Still, he could paint walls and furniture and replace the balding carpet. I'm wasting my time, planning. Winston would probably take to that suggestion as easily as he warmed up to Horace's hint to open the pool on the Friday before Memorial Day. It doesn't matter that it's hot enough now. The pool won't open early. And it doesn't matter that the motel could use a renovation. Winston thinks it's good enough.

That reminds me of the room with boxes piled in front of the window. I ask Violet about it. "Why don't you rent out Room Twelve?"

Violet peers sideways at me, then adds, "There wouldn't be enough space in there." She heads to the bathroom to clean. Subject closed. She has a funny way of avoiding certain topics about Winston. Have to admit, though, we're a pretty good team—Violet scrubbing toilets and me chasing away dust balls.

I run my cloth around the frame of a paint-by-numbers picture of a deer. I've dusted it before, but today I see the initials *D.H.* in the lower right-hand corner. My heart skips a beat. I holler, "My mom must have painted this!"

Violet comes out of the bathroom and looks at what I'm talking about. "No, Winston's wife did that."

"My grandmother?"

She lifts her eyebrows. "Well, yes, I guess that's right. She was your grandmother. She did a lot of those, but Winston got rid of them when she died. I think he forgot about this one."

"You knew my grandmother?"

"No, my folks and I moved here a few years after she passed away, but we met people who knew her. She sang in our church choir. They said she had the prettiest voice. She could sing alto and soprano on 'We're Marching to Zion.' There's a painting she did of the Last Supper in our fellowship hall. It must have taken her a long time to paint all those numbers. You know each number represents a color. Wonder how many numbers were in Jesus's beard?"

Violet is standing close to me now, examining my grandmother's deer picture.

"What does the *D* stand for?" I ask, even though my question reveals that Mom never told me anything about my grandmother.

"Her name was Dovie," Violet says. She turns around and heads back to her task. When she turns the fan on, it makes a loud, uneven racket, but I hear her when she calls out, "Grace! Dovie Grace!"

Grace. My mom gave me her mother's middle name, but she never told me about her. Not one thing except that time I caught her crying over that hymn on the radio. I think back to Grandparents Day at school. The teacher gave us a flyer about it to take home. I was only six, but because of what Dad had told me about how mentioning my grandparents would make Mom sad, I threw the flyer away in the garbage outside. If only I'd brought the flyer home. If only I'd given it to her and asked about my grandparents. Then I wouldn't have been a part of Mom and Dad's big pretend.

When we finish cleaning, I return the cart to the laundry room. After it's snug in place, I glance around the grounds and head over to Room 12. Once there, I peek through the window, trying to find a crack between the stacks of boxes.

Maybe my grandmother's paintings are inside one of them. Maybe my mother's things too.

"You won't find anything in there."

I nearly jump out of my skin.

"Caught you!" It's Roy and he's grinning. His nose and cheeks are sunburned, probably from his day at the lake. "Yep, there's nothing there but a bunch of old stuff."

"Why doesn't Winston get rid of it?"

Roy shrugs. "You know people and their junk. The reason I was looking for you was to ask if you want to go to the movies with my dad and me." His voice cracks at the "and me" part, and he stares down at his boots. This is the first time he's ever seemed shy. He always acts so confident.

I haven't seen a movie in a theater since my parents and I went to one last Christmas.

"That sounds fun," I tell him. "I'd better ask Winston first."

Winston is standing behind the register desk, reading a book about lobster fishermen in Maine. When I ask his permission to go to the movies, he looks up from the book. "Arlo is staying for the show?"

"Yes, that's what Roy said."

As if on cue, Arlo sticks his head in the office. "Okay if I take Stevie to the movies with Roy and me?"

Winston nods. "That will be okay. Don't know what you'd find interesting playing these days, though."

I rush to clean up, washing away the dirt but trying not to get my hair wet. After I change, Winston gives me some money.

"I don't need any," I tell him. I still have more than five hundred dollars.

"I owe you for cleaning the rooms."

"You don't have to do that."

"I do." He keeps holding out the money. It's an order.

I accept the cash and thank him. As I head out the door, Winston stops me.

"Stevie?"

I turn toward him. "Yes?"

"You're doing a good job cleaning the rooms."

"Thank you," I say. After I leave the office, I glance back. Winston is still watching me. But when he realizes I notice, he quickly looks down.

THE MOVIE IS PRETTY DUMB, mostly a guy flick with bathroom jokes, but I laugh at some of the stupid stuff anyway. I laugh until I look over at Roy and his dad laughing together. And I'm reminded I can never have that again.

Cultivate

Prepare the soil for planting

Chapter Thirteen

FRIDA MISSES A LOT OF CLASS, and today is one of those days. Even when she's here, she always leaves when Mrs. Crump falls asleep, somehow managing to return before she wakes up. I know what she does when she's gone because she always reeks of cigarette smoke. But where does she go?

"Stevie, I think it's important that you be familiar with the great American authors of the twentieth century. A good place to start would be with John—" Mrs. Crump is asleep. Just like every day after lunch, twelve thirty sharp. Little Esther's clocks could be set by her naps.

The window is open and a breeze flaps the lacy curtain. I sit there wondering, John who? What author was she going to mention? Then I realize how stupid I am, sitting here waiting for an old woman to wake up and teach me. I ease out of my chair. I tiptoe to the first floor, each step squeaking as my feet land on it. *Eek-kee! Eek-kee!* I listen for Mrs. Crump, but I can't hear her snoring. Each lock clicks as I twist it, but the door opens without a sound. I grab her umbrella in the corner and use it to prop open the door. That way, I can get back inside. Two o'clock is almost an hour and a half away from now. I feel giddy and rebellious. I feel like...Carmen. She'd be proud of me right now. She begged me to ditch P.E. class with her a few times. Believe me, I wanted to whenever we had to run laps. But for the most part I liked school, so I never said yes. Carmen called me Miss Goody Two-shoes. She teased me about it, but now I wish I'd skipped with her. I wonder where Carmen went when she walked off campus. She never told me and I never asked. Probably because I didn't want to know what I was missing.

Outside, the weather is perfect, the kind of day that reminds me of a New Mexico spring—the sun beating down on my back, the cool breeze blowing through my hair. But I just stand and stare at my reflection in the window. *What the heck am I doing?* Then I hear Carmen saying, "Don't be so perfect."

Before I chicken out, I dash down the porch steps and take off. I pass huge Victorian houses with towering magnolias and oaks in the front yards. Seeing all this green makes me realize how hungry I've been for it. If the motel were located in town, I'd walk these streets every day.

Door to door, pansies and red geraniums are popular picks. One house has a side kitchen garden with neatly planted salad greens of all sorts—radicchio, arugula, buttercrunch. Rosemary borders the raised beds. My thoughts head west. Mom called our kitchen garden a potager. That's what the French call theirs. Dad teased her about trying to make a hodgepodge garden sound fancy.

I imagine knocking on the door and my mother opening it, motioning me to her.

A woman pops out of the camellia bush in front of me. I jump back.

"Hi," she says. "Didn't mean to scare you."

"You didn't....I mean, I guess you did...a little." My breathing eases back into its regular pace. "Your yard is beautiful." I look down at the pots of pansies she's planting.

She smiles, and her crow's-feet deepen in her tanned skin. "Thank you, but it's not mine. I just do the landscaping."

"You're good."

"Thanks." She shades her eyes with her hand. "Hey, aren't you supposed to be in school?"

Maybe this is why I didn't skip before.

"I have a private teacher."

She seems to be waiting for more.

"It's recess." I hope I sound convincing. I clear my throat and ask, "How long have you been landscaping?"

"Oh, all my life." Her fingers tease the roots of the pansies, gently separating them, something I'd seen my parents do often. They did it as naturally as someone peels an orange. "My family owns Gavert's Plant Center on the edge of town. We sell plants, but we also do weddings and landscaping."

"Weddings?"

"We have a huge garden also. With a little white chapel. It's pretty popular with couples."

"I've been in the plant business all my life too."

"Really? Hey, are you one of my competitors?" She's grinning.

"My parents owned a little flower-and-herb farm in New Mexico."

"Did they sell it?"

"No. It's my farm now. They died." The words come out so easily, I surprise myself. *They died.*

She glances down at the flower bed but then quickly meets my gaze. "I'm sorry to hear that. I'll bet they were good folks. Plant people always are."

"You're right. I never thought about it until now. I mean, about plant people."

She pulls off one glove and stretches her arm over the low fence. "My name is Nancy. Nothing fancy about me, though."

"I'm Stevie. My parents named me after Stevie Nicks. They were both Fleetwood Mac fans." In less than two minutes, I've volunteered more about myself to this stranger than I have to anyone since the accident.

Before I know it, I'm removing the pansies from their pots, teasing the roots, and handing them to Nancy as she plants them in the ground. She chatters away about all the houses that she landscapes in the neighborhood. "A lot of old folks around here can't garden any longer. Big yards equal good business. Unfortunately, a lot of them can't afford our service. Some of them can barely pay their utility bills. These big old houses are energy hogs."

The sun is high in the sky. I glance at my watch and notice it's five until two. The church bell will chime soon. Brushing my hands off on my jeans, I tell her, "I'd better go. It was nice meeting you, Nancy."

"Same here, Stevie. Hope you'll drop by Gavert's. Be careful, though. We might put you to work."

I leave, passing all the homes I admired earlier. At the library, I begin to sprint until I reach Mrs. Crump's house. I ease the front door open and take two steps at a time. *Eek-kee, eek-kee, eek-kee.* When I arrive on the second floor, Mrs. Crump's head bobs like she's fighting sleep.

I settle into my chair just as the church bell chimes for the last time. Mrs. Crump dozes on. I drop a heavy encyclopedia on the floor. She opens her eyes and studies me a moment, then says, "Steinbeck gives us a close-up look at the Dust Bowl in *The Grapes of Wrath*. We'll start with him."

Mrs. Crump may be a narcoleptic, but she never fails to come back to the exact place she left off before her afternoon nap.

The phone rings a few minutes before Winston is due to pick me up.

"Do you want me to get it?" I ask.

"Don't be silly," Mrs. Crump says. She slowly pushes away from the table, takes hold of her cane, and *tap, tap, tap*s toward the telephone on the other side of the room. It's one of those old-fashioned phones that you see in movies, the kind attached to a curly cord. *Trring, trring. Tap, tap.* I have to sit on my hands to keep from hopping up and answering. *Trring, trring. Tap, tap.* Finally, she reaches the phone.

"Hello?" She pauses. "Hellooo?" She returns the phone to the cradle. "Seems they hung up."

Big surprise.

She starts back a few feet. *Trring, trring.* She turns around, picks up the phone. "Hello?"

After she hangs up, she says, "Winston is running late, but he wants you to wait for him at the Rise and

Shine Diner. He said he wouldn't be too long but to go ahead and have a snack if you'd like."

On my way to the square, I pass the house where I met Nancy earlier. She's already gone, but the borders are dense with pansies and red geraniums. I look out for her in each landscaped yard I pass. I don't see her, but I do see someone spray-painting the back porch of a house. It's Frida. She's shaking a can, and from the looks of it she's gone through a few colors already. The cans litter the dead grass around her. I can't tell what she's doing, but I suspect the owner will hate it if it's anything like her artwork in Crump's class. She doesn't notice me, so I pick up my pace and head toward the diner.

The Rise and Shine is slow, that lull between lunch and dinner. I buy two coconut cupcakes and settle at a table in front of a window. It's Friday, and I can tell that many of the passersby are tourists. The license plates confirm this—Arkansas, Washington, Oklahoma. The people get in and out of their cars with bags from the local shops. One man ties down an antique rocker in the back of his truck. These are the kind of people Winston is missing. If only he'd paint the motel, inside and out, and landscape. I close my eyes, imagining the motel painted sky blue, a Red Blaze climbing rose growing up a trellis. I pull out my geography notebook and, on the inside of its cover, sketch morning glories and trumpet vine covering a chain-link fence. I draw roses, phlox, herbs, and marigolds in the foreground. My heart beats faster, thinking of all the possibilities. I'm so caught up drawing rows of oregano and fennel, I don't see Winston come in.

"Ready?" he asks. He stands in front of me, looking down at the drawing. My head is so filled with garden plans, his beard has become a tangle of climbing roses. They twist all the way up one ear and out the other.

"Ready?" he asks again.

I slap my notebook closed and hand him a cupcake.

He holds it with a curled palm, as if it's a baby bird. "What's this?"

"A cupcake. For you."

Winston stares at it. "Thank you."

He keeps examining the cupcake like he has no idea how to go about eating it. Then he quickly yanks off the paper liner and pops the entire thing in his mouth.

Chapter Fourteen

On the drive home, I ask, "Can I cook dinner tonight?" I figure I have nothing to lose. Mom let me help with the cooking all the time.

Winston doesn't glance my way, but his fingers tap the steering wheel like he's playing piano keys. "Sure, if you want to go to all the trouble."

"Can we stop for groceries?"

"Of course." He turns my way, and his lips slide into a quick smile. Then, just like that, it's gone. But it feels like something is happening.

Winston makes a loop around the courthouse, which is in the center of the square, and heads toward the H-E-B store.

I pick out some cube steak. Most people have flour in

their pantry, but if Winston does, it's probably ages old. So I put a small package of flour into the cart. Eggs. I think of the chickens and wonder how they're doing at Angelina Cruz's. Milk, butter, canola oil. Potatoes to make on the side. I almost forget fixings for a salad. I haven't eaten anything green in a while. In the produce section, I dream of the row of greens growing in our old garden. Not iceberg, but arugula, romaine, and buttercrunch lettuce. Maybe when it gets cooler next fall, I can plant some among the flowers. I grab a lime for some dressing.

The cashier is wearing a purple headband, and it makes me think of coneflowers. When the lady in front of us opens her purse, a butterfly bush covered in hot-pink blooms shoots up and reaches the height of a beach umbrella. I swear eating all this soup has made me delusional.

BACK AT THE APARTMENT, Winston is studying his albums. They look really old, older than Mom's and Dad's. "Haven't listened to these in a long time."

"Why don't you play them?"

"I don't have a record player anymore."

"I have one."

"I noticed that."

"Would you like to use it?"

"Thanks. If you don't mind?"

I head to my room, wondering why he has all those albums and no record player. Winston meets me outside my room and takes the player from me. He looks down at it and says, "Still in pretty good shape."

We'd had the record player forever. I thought my parents bought it after they got married, but the way Winston is gently wiping off the turntable with a soft cloth, it makes me wonder if it was his.

"You sure you want to cook?"

"Getting tempted to use the can opener, huh?" I couldn't resist, but I instantly regret it.

To my surprise, though, Winston laughs. "You don't care much for my menus?"

I stay quiet, because even though I want us to get along, I want to hear him say something about Mom. And until he does, I don't think we can be anything but two people sharing the same address. Number 1 at the Texas Sunrise Motel.

Winston puts on an album while I quarter the potatoes before dropping them into a pot. My fingers know the recipe by heart.

The song's *pop-bebop* matches the sound of the boiling water. Winston is stretched out on the couch with his shoes off. There's a hole in the heel of one of his socks.

I cover the steak with waxed paper and pound on it with a soup can. It feels good to hit something. Winston seems to notice. He peers from around an album cover, smiling.

"Guess you're kind of tired of my old standby?"

"What?" Then I get it. "Well, let's just say if Campbell's needs someone for a new commercial, you're their man."

Winston hides his face behind the album. The saxophone moans a lonesome piece, and I expect to hear it again, but the sax never returns to that string of notes. Sometimes the music sounds like plates breaking. I'll stick to rock and roll.

After the steaks have cooked, I sprinkle flour into the drippings and slowly add the milk to make the gravy. Every once in a while, I feel Winston's eyes on me. I wonder what he's thinking. Is he wishing there wasn't a girl in his kitchen cooking, a girl he's now responsible for? Is he wishing he could get on with his quiet life of Campbell's soup and two newspapers?

When we settle down at the table to eat, Winston studies his meal. I'm proud of it. Earlier I sliced a piece of my steak to make sure it tasted right. And the good cream gravy will make anyone forget the lumps in the mashed potatoes.

"Chicken-fried steak?"

"You've had it before?"

He lets out a snort. "Honey, Texas invented chicken-fried steak."

My body goes numb. He called me *honey*. But he says it the way a waitress might say it to a customer. To someone she doesn't know well or even care about.

"Where did you learn..." He stops, because of course he already knows.

I answer anyway. "My mom taught me. Maybe she learned it from her mom?"

Now I'm asking, but Winston isn't answering. He's busy eating. And I think he likes it.

After we eat, Winston tells me he'll do the dishes since I cooked, and I let him. In my room, I stretch out on the bed. Today was my best day in Little Esther, but all at once I feel homesick. I've got to get back to the farm.

Chapter Fifteen

FRIDA SOMEHOW MANAGES to attend class all week. Maybe someone caught her doing graffiti. Maybe she's grounded and her punishment is going to school. She seems different, though. Happier. Like she learned she won the lottery. When Mrs. Crump tells us to write, Frida actually does. But she won't share when Mrs. Crump asks if she wants to read what she wrote. And when Mrs. Crump asks me, I don't either. Frida and I are two private vessels on an ocean.

Sometimes I wonder what it would be like to be her friend. She's not that much different from Carmen. Neither one of them likes school, and both of them love skipping. Except Frida never asks me to skip with her.

She finishes her work, then takes out a pad and starts drawing.

I'm getting itchy to skip during Mrs. Crump's nap. I want to explore her neighbors' gardens, find out what grows easily here. Maybe I'd run into Nancy. But Frida doesn't make a move to leave when Mrs. Crump starts to snore, so I decide to stay too. *Chicken. Cluck, cluck, cluck.*

SATURDAY, Winston is busy making a list—a list of things that must be done while he's away at the New Orleans Jazz Festival. He said he goes every year. It's kind of been a jazz fest around here lately. Music hasn't stopped playing at the apartment since Winston put on that album last weekend. That's the way it was at home, except I'm not familiar with this kind of music. Last week, I learned about Art Tatum and Dizzy Gillespie. I doubt Winston even knows who Led Zep, Barry Manilow, or the Beatles are. I'm thankful Winston's jazz sounds nothing like my parents' music. It would kill me to hear those old songs.

I've been making my own list, a list of plants to buy at Gavert's Plant Center. I want the garden to be a surprise for Winston.

Winston will be gone for six days. While he's away, Violet will come in early and work more hours, and Arlo will cover the night shift. A lot can happen in six days. When he returns, he'll see what a big difference a garden makes. Maybe he'll even be inspired to paint the motel.

A couple of days before he leaves, Winston says, "You'll be staying with Violet while I'm away."

"Can't I stay here? If I have a problem, Arlo will be here," I tell him.

"Violet lives in town, so you'll only have to walk a block to Mrs. Crump's house."

When I leave the office to scout a place for the garden, I hear banging and cursing coming from the laundry room. It's Horace. He's pounding on the washing machine.

I try to lighten his mood. "May she rest in peace. Now Winston will have to buy a new one."

"Winston's not going to sacrifice one dime to improve this place." Horace spits the words. He doesn't even glance at me. He reverses his wheelchair so fast, I have to jump out of his way. He moves quickly toward the office. I follow him. I don't want to miss the action. When

Horace reaches the door, I open it for him but decide to wait outside. Horace's voice is loud, and I can see through the window in the door.

"For Pete's sake, Winston, get a new washing machine!"

Winston rolls his eyes and grabs the walkie-talkie. "Arlo, Bertha's on the blink again."

The walkie-talkie crackles, and Arlo's voice comes through. "I'm on it."

"Arlo is great, but he's no miracle worker," Horace says. "Sears is having a sale on Maytags."

"It's getting fixed," Winston says.

Horace grips the arms of his wheelchair, causing his biceps to bulge. "How are me and Ida going to make it to Florida without clean clothes?"

He sharply turns his chair around and leaves. For the second time, I hop out of his way so the wheelchair doesn't run over my toes.

"Pensacola?" I'm excited for him and Ida. They're finally going on a honeymoon.

"Soon," he snaps. He keeps on moving, muttering under his breath, using what Violet calls Horace's sailor talk.

They aren't really going to Florida anytime soon. He's just angry.

Horace returns to the laundry room and pulls the wet clothes out of the washing machine. He wrings out a shirt, letting the water splatter on the floor.

I race over to help him, but he snaps, "I've got it!"

He stops what he's doing. "I'm sorry, Stevie. Your grandfather will squeeze blood out of a turnip or die trying."

I'm mad at Winston too, not because he won't replace Bertha but because of my being sent to Violet's house like I'm a little kid. And he's not saying anything about what happened to Mom. Doesn't he know how cruel that is?

"Winston is being rotten," I say. It feels good to have someone who's mad at him too. "He's selfish."

Horace's face softens, and he stares at me like somebody slapped him. "Stevie, Winston is cheap. I'll say that. But he's not selfish. This was the fourth place I looked at that would give Ida and me a place at a decent price. Not only did Winston offer us something we could afford, he had Arlo enlarge our doorways and renovate the bathroom. He gave up two hotel rooms so we could even have a kitchen." He points at something. "He added that ramp right outside our door."

"He did?"

"Yeah," Horace says. "There's a heart in that man's chest. Hard to find sometimes, but it's there, believe me."

He spins his wheelchair around and takes off in the direction of his apartment, adding, "He's still cheap, though."

While I search around the motel for my future garden, I think about what Horace just said. What happened between Winston and Mom? Was it Dad?

I'm thinking about this so much, I don't even know how I end up at the motel sign. At the sign's base, the phlox is taller now—still not ready to bloom, but it's as if it's saying, *Here.*

Chapter Sixteen

VIOLET'S PINK VICTORIAN HOME needs a little tender loving care too. Patches of flaking paint and crooked gingerbread trim remind me of a three-tiered wedding cake made during someone's first day at a bakery. Although the grass is cut, volunteer crepe myrtles have invaded the yard, popping up in random places. If they aren't pulled up soon, they will grow into trees in no time. The grass is polka-dotted with yellow dandelions. Someone needs to take care of her lawn. Even so, the huge house looks like the kind of place where rich people live. Seeing it makes me wonder why Violet works at the motel.

Winston must read my mind. "Violet's parents left her the house, and I hope a lot of money. Those old things cost a small fortune in utilities."

I remember what Nancy said about that. Now I realize just because someone lives in a big house doesn't mean they're rich.

Violet meets us wearing her Island Paradise dress—a cream background with plate-size pink hibiscus. She's also wearing a gold chain necklace that's just like the one a guest left behind. Inside, an explosion of floral chintz covers the furniture and hangs around the windows. Pink and purple dominate, but there's yellow, orange, and plenty of green too.

"It's Greer Garson week!" she squeaks, bouncing on her toes. "Back-to-back Greer movies. We're going to have fun!"

Winston raises his eyebrows. "Greer Garson? They still show her old movies?"

"You need cable, Winston," Violet says.

"Guess I won't be seeing Greer Garson anytime soon," he tells her.

"You could watch John Wayne movies." Violet says it like she's dangling a mouse in front of a cat.

"I didn't like those when they were in the theaters," Winston says.

"My dad loved John Wayne," Violet says softly.

Winston glances at his watch. Then he reaches out and taps my shoulder. "You take care."

It's the closest he's come to showing me any affection. He leaves through the front door, but I rush over and catch the knob before it closes.

"Have a good time," I tell him.

He turns, startled.

And then I reach over and give him a quick hug.

Winston opens his mouth as if he wants to say something, but nothing comes out. He lifts his hand in a quick wave.

While I watch Winston make his way to the van, I remember how whenever I'd go anywhere for more than a few hours, my parents gave me a send-off that made me homesick before I'd even left. I hope Winston is careful driving all the way to New Orleans. It's going to take him all day. He's old, and New Orleans is a big city. And now I'm wondering why I care and why I bothered hugging him. Maybe because I've been thinking about how Winston made all the changes at the hotel for Horace and Ida. Maybe, like Horace said, "there's a heart in that man's chest."

Violet joins me on the porch, and together we wave

to the back of Winston's van. When it vanishes from sight, Violet says, "Let's make grilled-cheese sandwiches. We can have popcorn later, when the movie comes on."

Violet pulls some bread and Velveeta from a deep pantry and places them on the marble countertop. Even the kitchen hasn't escaped her pastel touch. Pink Depression glass plates are stacked inside glass-front cabinets.

"Tonight Greer is in *Mrs. Miniver*," she says. "Have you seen it?"

"No, I don't think so."

An hour later, we're sitting on the couch with big bowls of buttered popcorn and a box of tissues between us. For some reason, wiping tears away feels good.

Chapter Seventeen

I WAKE UP TO A PERIWINKLE CEILING and angels smiling down on me. It takes me a second to remember where I am. I'm not at the Rockasita or the Texas Sunrise Motel. I'm at Violet's. I wonder if she painted the ceiling. If she did, she's not half bad unless you count the angel with a big smile and the big dots on the cheeks that I guess are supposed to be dimples.

After dressing, I head toward the kitchen, hoping to find Violet. I'm hungry, but I feel funny snooping around for something to eat. Sunshine streams in through the kitchen window over the sink, creating a hazy beam across the room. Since Violet isn't here, I pull out a chair and wait. After a while, I wonder if she's already left for the motel, but her green Volkswagen convertible is parked out front in the driveway. The top is down, and I think nothing of it until I realize it's raining. A sun shower. I loved when that happened back home, because sometimes if the sun was low enough in the sky, a rainbow would follow. Mom would say, "Go fetch your pot of gold." I watch the drops slide down the windshield. Violet's car is going to turn into a pond if someone doesn't pull the top up.

I rush outside and try to raise the convertible top. I pull and pull, but it won't budge. The rain is picking up, so I look for a magic button to push. I give up and honk the horn.

"Oh, dear!" Violet is at the front door. She's wearing a shower cap and a large plastic garbage sack as a poncho. Barefooted, she rushes to the car, gets in, and puts the key in the ignition. She pushes a button, and the top slowly rises and shuts in place.

For some dumb reason, I stand close by and watch helplessly. By the time I head to the porch, I'm drenched.

"Oh, Stevie, I'm sorry. Blame it on Greer. This happens every time I watch one of her movies. I forget my routine. Stay here a second and I'll get you a towel." Before walking away, she pulls off the shower cap and the garbage sack and throws them on the porch. She's fully dressed for work.

The rain has already turned to a slow drizzle, as if Mother Nature was playing a prank. I hope it rains like this after we plant our garden. Then it dawns on me: I haven't taken care of the "we" part yet. I need to ask Arlo and Roy soon, tomorrow at the latest. I have the money to buy the plants, but I'll need Arlo to take me to the nursery and back to the motel with them. And I'll never be able to clear a space for the garden and plant it by myself in time for Winston's return.

Violet comes back with a big fluffy towel and helps me dry off. "Your hair is so long. It's going to take forever to dry. Do you want to use my hair dryer?"

"Sounds like a good idea." I forgot mine at the motel.

A few minutes later, I'm sitting in Violet's dusty-pink bathroom under a turquoise bubble-head dryer, the kind I've only seen in old movies, being used by ladies with spiky rollers. The dryer's hum is loud and the air blowing on my scalp is hot. I sure hope I'm ready in time for Mrs. Crump's lessons.

Violet bends down and hollers in my face. "Can I get you some toast? Toast makes everything better."

By the time I've eaten the wheat toast with butter and orange marmalade, the top part of my hair is dry. And I agree. Toast is comforting and almost as tasty as blueberry Pop-Tarts.

"I'm sorry I can't take you to Mrs. Crump, but I'm already running late. Arlo is probably wondering where I am. If you want, you can take my bicycle."

"You have a bike?"

"Yes, I haven't ridden it in a long time, but I'll put it on the porch if you decide to use it. I'll even leave the helmet." Violet studies her image in the tall foyer mirror and puts on a quick coat of lipstick. Then she heads outside. "Have a good day!"

I loved my first bike. Mom and Dad took me to the park near the plaza and I rode until they begged me to stop so we could go home. It'll be fun to ride again.

Before leaving for Mrs. Crump's, I triple-check the front door to make sure it's locked. The rain has completely stopped, and the sun is shining so bright, it casts a haze around the yard. Leaning against a porch column is a pink banana-seat bicycle with a wicker basket fastened to the front of the handlebars. The shiny purple helmet's strap is looped over one of the handles.

I guess it has been a long time since Violet has ridden. Maybe since Pluto stopped being called a planet. I should leave the bike and dash off to Mrs. Crump's before the rain decides to return. But I can't quit staring at that bike.

After I outgrew my first bike, I never rode again. I don't know why. I guess I wasn't interested anymore. They say once you ride a bike, you can always ride one. I look toward the street. It's empty and quiet.

I throw my backpack in the basket and climb on. I try on the helmet. It feels like my brains are being squeezed into a pulp. I leave it on the porch. The bike seat is a little too low for my long legs, and when I pedal, my knees narrowly miss the handlebars. It's a wobbly start, but in a moment I'm off the curb and onto the street. It feels good to glide through the puddles in the low spots. The fresh smell of rain reminds me of how in Taos rain arrived almost every afternoon around four o'clock. Gentle and quick. Mom called it a spit bath. Until this morning, I didn't realize how much I missed the rain's daily visit.

Mrs. Crump's house is around the corner and up a block. An old white pickup truck, coming from the opposite direction, slows as it nears me. When it stops, my heart pounds and I pick up my pace.

"Hey, Stevie!"

I look over and discover Nancy, the landscape lady, in the driver's seat. She's wearing a baseball cap with GAVERT'S PLANT CENTER on it.

I slam on the brakes and almost fall. "Hi, Nancy!"

"Like your wheels. Are you at recess again?" She says it with a chuckle and a wink.

"No, I'm on my way to class."

"Looks like you've been swimming."

I touch my wet ends. "Long story."

"Need a lift? You could put your bicycle in the back of the truck."

"Thanks, but I'm almost there. The bike isn't mine."

Nancy grins. "Hey, I'm not judging. Study hard. Hope to see you around soon. You never know. I might put you to work." She drives off, and I watch until she disappears down the street. At least it wasn't Frida and her mom. I pedal the princessmobile the rest of the way to Mrs. Crump's. I'm hoping Frida is already there so she won't see me, but then I hear a motorcycle. Mrs. James pulls onto the driveway. A bunch of sponge rollers cover her head. Frida gets off quickly and walks past me. She looks down like she's embarrassed. I figure it's because of the rollers. I'd be horrified if my mom left the house like that. For a second, I forgot Mom is dead. And that realization is killing me. I'd give anything to have Mom here with rollers or blue hair, or even bald.

Frida is waiting for me on the front porch. She's standing tall in her cocky, don't-mess-with-me pose. "Hey, Barbie! Did Ken take the keys to your pink convertible today?"

I guess a pink bicycle with a banana seat trumps a mom in rollers for Most Nerdy Drop-Off.

DURING MRS. CRUMP'S NAP, I keep working on my algebra. Even Frida is doing hers. She's nibbling at her eraser as she clicks away at the calculator. I'm still wondering what she's up to with this good-girl routine. When I finish my work, I go to the other side of the room. One shelf is filled with leather-bound photo albums with the years typed on labels and in chronological order. They take up an entire shelf, from 1960 to the current year.

Mom would have attended sometime in the 1990s, but I have no idea when she started with Mrs. Crump. Did she ever go to school? If so, did something happen to make my grandfather take her out?

Frida stares at me across the room. Without thinking, I snap, "Mind your own business." I regret it as soon as I say it.

Frida goes back to punching numbers.

We've exchanged attitudes. What am I thinking? Bad girls don't think looking through someone's photo albums is a big deal. I open up the 1994 album and thumb through photos of European trips. Most of this one is of places in Paris—the Eiffel Tower, the Louvre, the Moulin Rouge. Another album is filled with pictures of Mexico City.

I study the dozing woman in front of me. Mrs. Crump may be old, but she's had adventures. These photo albums prove it. Her head rests on her right shoulder, and her chin melts into her face and the folds of her neck. This may seem strange, but I think her wrinkles are beautiful. I loved Angelina Cruz's wrinkles too. "A line for every year," she'd sometimes say. "Heartache and joy, it's all there."

As Mrs. Crump softly snores and Frida does math, I pull album after album off the shelf, returning each one, as I finish, to its proper place. The pictures are interesting, but I don't see my mom in any of them.

The church bell chimes. Frida looks at my empty chair and then in my direction. I quickly return the last album to the left side of the shelf and hurry back to my chair. I make it in time. Frida claps like she's applauding my race to the finish line.

Mrs. Crump's eyes open just as I realize I replaced the book in the wrong order.

Chapter Eighteen

IT'S THE SECOND NIGHT at Violet's, and we've watched six Greer Garson movies. We decide to get in our night-clothes and stay up late to watch *Blossoms in the Dust*. I'm enjoying the film, until the part with all those orphans when I realize I'm one too. Carmen would get a kick out of me watching these old movies. She'd probably think they were corny, but I don't care. I'm becoming a big classic-movie fan. Not as big as Violet, though. She's thinking of going on a TCM cruises. Old movies play around the clock on the ship, and people go to parties dressed up like their favorite movie characters.

"If I go," Violet says, "I'm dressing up like Marilyn Monroe in *The Prince and the Showgirl*."

While I slip on my pajama bottoms and Dad's Pink

Floyd T-shirt, I plot how I'll get Mrs. Crump's photo album back to the right spot. Tomorrow I'll move it as soon as she falls asleep.

Back in the parlor, Violet is thumbing through a well-worn copy of *Good Housekeeping*. Her nightgown seems familiar. Then I realize it's the nightgown left behind in the first room we cleaned together. She doesn't even seem to care that I might recognize it.

"That little rain we had this morning didn't account for much moisture," she says, examining her face in the gigantic mirror in the foyer. "We need to do something for our parched skin and hair."

I glance at my image in the mirror and discover I have a pimple on the tip of my nose.

A few minutes later, we pile gobs of mayonnaise on our roots and pull the excess down to the ends. Violet twists Saran Wrap around our heads, forming turbans. Then she mixes plain yogurt and cucumber pulp and smears the concoction on our skin. We smell like the salad bar section of Western Sizzlin. But the mask feels refreshing on my face.

While we wait for the movie to begin, Violet asks, "What did your mother look like?"

I'm startled by her question. After a long pause, I settle on, "She was beautiful and kind to everybody." Then I add, "She had curly blond hair and blue eyes."

"Like your eyes?"

"That's what most people say." Everyone but Winston.

"I knew she'd be nice," Violet says.

"Why?" I expect her to say something like, *Because you are.*

Instead she says, "Because she's named after a flower. You can't have a name like Daisy—or Violet or Rose, for that matter—and be a disagreeable person. It would be contradictory, and you'd always be lopsided. Although I guess there are a few lopsided people in this world with flower names. I know one. That grumpy cashier at the Dollar Store, her name is Lilee, but she uses a double *e* on the end." Violet carefully scratches her scalp with an index finger.

The time seems right to reveal my big plan. "Violet, how would you like to see some real flowers at the motel?"

"I used to bring in a vase of flowers, but Winston said they'd cause customers to sneeze."

This might be a bigger challenge than I'd thought. "A garden out front will get the hotel more attention, and then we'll have more customers."

"Oh, I don't know about that. Seems like most people just head on to Dallas. We get mostly traveling salesmen who have to pay their own expenses." The movie begins playing the opening credits. She pulls her knees to her chest and sighs with glee. Then she adds, "But I'll think about it."

It's a start. Then I ask her something I've been wondering about for a while now. "How does Winston stay in business? How does Winston make enough money to live?"

"He made a bunch of money in the stock market. That's what I hear, anyway."

If that was really true, why would he keep the motel? Then, as if she reads my thoughts, Violet says, "He uses the motel for a tax write-off. That's what Horace thinks."

The opening music is starting.

Once again, Greer makes Violet cry. She gently dabs her eye with a handkerchief, careful not to disturb her beauty mask.

I'm not paying attention to the movie. I'm thinking about the garden and what it will take to convince Violet and Arlo that it's the right thing to do.

Chapter Nineteen

THE FIRST FEW MINUTES I open my eyes, I think the angels on the ceiling are really floating around on the clouds. Another morning at Violet's. Just when I'm thinking I can get ready early so that she can drive me to Mrs. Crump's, I discover the bike at the foot of my bed with a giant red bow. A card is attached. *To Stevie, A just-because gift. From, Violet.*

Violet meets me outside the bedroom door. "Oh, I wanted to see your expression when you opened your eyes."

"Gosh, Violet, you shouldn't have." She really shouldn't have.

"Well, since you rode it yesterday and I figured that I'm never getting on that thing again, you should have it."

"I'm not sure what to say."

She stares at me, waiting.

"Thank you."

"You're welcome!" She hugs me and squeezes hard. "I loved that bike, but I love giving it to someone who appreciates it."

I stare at the banana seat, the little bell, the wicker basket. Any nine-year-old girl would love seeing this pink number under her Christmas tree.

Violet's hands are locked together like she's trying to keep her excitement from bursting into a fireworks show. How could I ever tell Violet I don't want the bike? I don't bother asking for a ride to Mrs. Crump's.

FRIDA ISN'T IN CLASS TODAY, and I don't know why but I kind of miss her. At least I'll have a chance to put the photo album back without having to explain it to her. Mrs. Crump falls asleep almost right after her last bite of lunch. I wait a couple of minutes before easing out of my chair and moving toward the bookcase. Then I read the albums' spines—1993, 1994, 1995. I check the years again. I must have been mistaken. I must have returned it to the right place. Or maybe somehow Frida did. She's so sneaky.

Instead of planning the garden or taking a walk about town, I go back to the table, open my algebra book, and do the next lesson. Math is my least favorite subject, but the problems calm my nerves and distract me. Soon the clock sounds and Mrs. Crump shakes her head like a dog after a swim. She waits for me to finish the formula.

"Stevie?" She reaches across the table and touches my hand with her cold fingers. "Would you like to know about your mother when she was with me?"

My skin prickles.

"Yes," I whisper.

She smiles softly. "Daisy was creative and intelligent. It's not difficult for me to see you're her child."

"Did she ever go to the school in town?"

"Yes, she was there until her mother died. Then your grandfather hired me to teach her. She was only with me about a year."

I want to ask why Mom had to come to Mrs. Crump, but I'm afraid the question might sound as if I don't think she's a good teacher.

She must have read my thoughts, because she adds, "I'm not such a bugbear, am I?"

"Oh, no! You're a wonderful teacher," I tell her, even though I have no idea what a bugbear is. But my thoughts float back to the day Roy told me about the school letting her go.

She chuckles. "Well, I'm not sure everyone would agree with that."

I wonder if Mom left when she met my dad.

"Daisy was also a wonderful photographer," Mrs. Crump says.

"She took pictures back then?"

"Yes, she did. I used to like taking pictures myself."

I think about the neat black-and-white photographs in her albums. Of course, I can't mention that or she'd know I was snooping through them.

"I took a few classes," she tells me, "but I never moved past amateur status."

"Did you teach Mom?"

"Oh, I passed along what I'd learned. Your mom had natural talent. I have something you might like." She pushes the atlas aside. Underneath is a folder. She hands it to me.

DAISY HIMMEL is written in large letters across the folder. I open it and find a makeshift book with a photograph of a window on the cover.

I'm captivated by my mother's handwriting underneath the picture. It looks a little different from what I remember, bigger and loopier. Her *i*'s are dotted with hearts. I've done that before. When I look at the photo closely, I realize why it looks so familiar. It's the window in my bedroom. Her bedroom. The shade is pulled up, and the pull with the circle dangles from it.

Mrs. Crump tells me, "I kept a copy because I was certain she'd be a famous photographer one day."

"She loved taking pictures." I can tell by the way Mrs. Crump smiles that she is pleased. We're like spies trading information.

"She had this old camera that took film," I say. "A couple of years ago she traded it in for a digital."

Mrs. Crump flinches a little. "Did the old one look like that one?"

My eyes follow her finger, which is pointing to the top shelf of her bookcase. It's filled with knickknacks. The camera is next to a small sombrero.

"It looked almost exactly like that one."

"Well, I'm glad she was still taking pictures."

I'm starting to put things together. "Did you give that camera to her?"

"I wasn't using it anymore. And I had the other one. Which, believe it or not, at one time was the newest thing since sliced bread."

I feel awful about telling her that Mom traded it in. "Mom loved her old camera, though. She was pretty stubborn about changing it. But developing film really adds up."

She chuckles. "Oh, goodness, I've been around long enough to see a lot of things come and go."

"Can I borrow the book with Mom's pictures?"

"Consider it yours."

"Thank you, Mrs. Crump." I start to peek but quickly close it and tuck the book back into the folder. I want to look at it alone, to study each picture carefully.

Mrs. Crump leans in closer. "Now may I ask you a question?"

"Sure?"

"Was Daisy happy?"

Mrs. Crump blurs in front of me until she is a multicolored spot. With the back of my wrist, I try to catch a tear before it falls, but I fail. It lands on the folder.

"Yes," I manage to say. "We were all happy."

"I'm so glad to know that," she says. Then she scoots away from the table and *tap, tap, tap*s to her desk for the tissue box.

I have one last question. "Did you ever meet my dad?"

"No, honey. I'm sorry, but I lost track of your mom after she finished and I went on the African safari."

"You went on a safari?" I try to envision her riding an elephant.

Mrs. Crump tilts her head. "You must not have made it through all my albums."

Sow

Plant or scatter seeds in the earth

Chapter Twenty

VIOLET PICKS ME UP from her house at three thirty sharp. She needs to work at the desk for a couple more hours.

"How's the bike?" she asks.

"Great," I tell her, wondering how I'm ever going to be able to get rid of it. For a second, I wish I was the kind of person who could ditch the bike.

"Have you rung the bell yet? I used to love to ride up and down the street, ringing my bell. Everybody would wave from their front porches."

I could never ditch the bike.

When we arrive at the motel, I head toward my room and settle cross-legged on my bed. I open Mom's photography book. At first I think I'll look at every single picture. Then I change my mind because there're only a few. I'll look at one picture a day. Each one will be like a visit with Mom. I'll take my time and learn what I can from them. I open to the first page. Shot from above, the picture shows someone's legs from her knees down to her shoes. The legs must be Mom's. The shoes are small, and Mom had little feet. I count the freckles on her knees, the only place she had any. Her calves are slender like mine, only hers are pale. I roll up my jeans and look for freckles. But there are none. I stare at that picture for a long time before closing the book and tucking it back into the folder.

It's already four o'clock. If I'm ever going to plant a garden, I need to convince Arlo to take me to Gavert's Plant Center. And I'll need his help. Roy's too. When I first started planning the garden, I thought of doing the whole thing myself. But that was stupid. Making a new garden is hard work. This is a three-day weekend, so it's perfect.

Arlo is cleaning the lint out of the dryer in the laundry room. It's especially humid today. The room smells musty and soapy. The words rush from my mouth as I share my plans with him and explain that I need his help.

He pauses a long time, making a baseball from the gray lint. Finally, he says, "This means a lot to you, doesn't it, Stevie?"

I nod.

"What the heck—Winston has fired me twice before. What's one more time?"

"He's fired you?"

He slowly grins. "I'm still here."

When Roy peers from around the linen-closet door, I jump. He's wearing a red cap, and I don't recognize him right away. He laughs. "You can count on me for the job. Winston's never fired me. I need practice."

And though they don't seem worried about it, now I am. "I don't want you to get fired. I just thought it would be a nice surprise."

Arlo rubs his chin. "Uh, Stevie, just so you know, Winston doesn't much like surprises, good or bad. He's what you'd call a creature of habit."

I think Arlo is wrong about this, though. Winston will like the garden.

In Taos, we had a neighbor who said she wished she could snap her fingers and her greenhouse would be clean. She'd let it pile up with dead plants and empty pots over the years. One day while she was visiting her sister out of town, Mom, Dad, and I sneaked over and cleaned it out. Then we stacked the terra-cotta pots in neat piles. It looked like a page in a garden magazine.

When she returned home, she was so happy, she cried. She kept saying, "You did this for me?"

The funny thing is, it took us only a couple of hours. That day, I realized doing small things for people can be a big gift.

Back at Violet's house, I can't fall asleep. The garden is heavy in my thoughts, and I'm excited thinking about how, with Arlo and Roy helping, the garden is going to happen. I toss and turn, and eventually I flick on the bedside lamp. It's after midnight, so I decide to look at one more of Mom's pictures.

The second-page photograph shows part of a sign— **VERT'S** printed in large dark letters. Below is *nter* in small italics. I try to think like Vanna White, that lady on the game show *Wheel of Fortune* who flips around the squares with letters that spell out phrases. Nothing comes to me, even after I go through the entire alphabet, but I'm finally sleepy.

THE NEXT MORNING, I crawl into Arlo's truck and sit between him and Roy. A lot has happened since the first time I rode in this truck, and I've only been here about a month.

"We're ready to get fired," Roy says with his one-dimple smirk.

He must see my worry, because he winks at me. "I'm kidding! Anyway, if Winston doesn't like it, I can always be a paperboy."

Arlo glances around. "Just where are you thinking of making the garden?"

"Beneath and around the sign."

"The Texas Sunset Motel sign?"

I nod.

"Interesting," Arlo says.

Maybe he thought I was going to make the garden in the back of the motel. That wouldn't do any good. The garden will attract customers. It can't be hidden like a secret garden.

A few minutes later, we're heading toward the edge of town. Fountain grass lines the road leading to the parking lot. Gavert's Plant Center's sweep of color makes my heart beat faster—red geraniums, salmon salvia, purple coneflowers, roses of all kinds. I plan to spend every penny in my wallet. Four hundred and sixty dollars. Well, maybe I should keep a little for pocket change.

When we get out of the truck, the sweet scent of honeysuckle vine floats around us. A prickle travels from my elbow to my wrist. This smells just like the farm in spring. The FOR SALE sign flashes in my thoughts, but I push it away. *The farm will wait for me.*

Arlo gets a flatbed cart. "What's it going to be, boss?"

"We'll need topsoil, compost, and mulch," I tell him.

"How many bags?" Roy asks.

I should have figured that out before now. Just as I'm about to admit that I don't know, a familiar voice says, "Hello, Stevie-Named-After-Stevie-Nicks!"

Nancy wears a green apron with GAVERT'S across the bib and yellow gardening gloves. "Got spring fever?"

"Hi, Nancy. This is—"

"Arlo and Roy Fulton," she says, holding her hand out to Arlo. "How the heck are you, boys?" She gives him a firm shake.

"You know each other?" I ask.

Roy laughs. "This isn't Dallas. We know everybody in this town."

"So what are you three outlaws up to?" Nancy asks.

"We're building a garden," Roy says. "A Texas Sunrise Motel garden."

"Oh...," Nancy says. "Wait a second, Stevie. Is Winston your grandfather?"

I nod.

"Daisy is your mom?!" She pauses a second, then says, "Oh, gosh, Stevie. I'm so sorry. I didn't know about... Your mom was a nice girl. I'd graduated by the time she even got to high school, but everyone liked her."

A lump is growing in my throat. I want to ask a million questions about Mom. I clear my throat, but that dang lump won't go away.

Arlo comes to my rescue. "We're trying to figure out how much topsoil and compost we need."

"How big of a garden are you planting?" Nancy asks.

Arlo looks at me. I still can't speak.

Roy walks about, forming an oblong-shaped outline. "Oh, about yay-big."

"I think I can fix you up. Plus, you can always come back for more if it's not enough."

She starts handing over to us sacks of soil and compost. We pile them on the flatbed cart.

I swallow and manage to speak. "We need mulch too."

"Of course!" Nancy says. "Gotta have mulch."

When I pick up a shovel, Arlo says, "We've got a couple of those."

"A hoe?" I ask.

"Nope, not that."

"There's a lot of grass to remove," I say, grabbing three, one for each of us. But when I notice the price, I put two back.

"You mean weeds," Roy says. "When you mow them, they sorta resemble grass."

We pile another flatbed cart with plants. I'm overwhelmed with the choices, and I choose two needlepoint hollies. They're small now, but they'll grow and can be the background of the garden, with the knockout roses and some dwarf mock orange in the front. I remember how Dad would say, "Flowers are our business, but the evergreens are for us. They give us something to look at all year round."

We grab a few Shasta daisies, agapanthus, marigold seeds, and about a dozen fountain grass plants. Their amber plumes will wave to the cars from the road. I look long and hard at a concrete birdbath, but it costs eighty bucks.

"That's an awesome birdbath, isn't it?" Nancy is standing behind me with the notepad. "I love how it's shaped like a giant daisy. And it's shallow enough for little birds." There probably won't be enough money left for that.

After Nancy writes up our purchases, the guys head to the truck with the carts and I head over to the register to pay. "Were you friends with my mom?" It keeps amazing me how I can talk to Nancy about anything.

"No. When you're a kid, a few years' difference in age can seem like decades. But she was really nice. I guess you know she loved taking pictures. She sometimes took pictures at the garden center. So should I invoice Winston for all this?"

"No, I'm getting it." I pull out my wallet and take out the hundred-dollar bills.

Nancy takes the cash and gives me the change. She motions one of the workers over and tells him, "See that truck with those two guys in the parking lot? Load up that birdbath for them."

"What?" I'm not sure what to say.

"In honor of your mom," Nancy says.

That lump comes back big time, so I give Nancy a quick hug. "My pleasure," she says.

At the truck, I tell the guys, "How about ice cream? My treat."

Roy slips his arm around my shoulders. "I'll let my rich new friend treat me to a milkshake." He quickly removes his arm, but I can still feel his touch.

"Your almost-broke new friend," I tell him. As we pull away, I stare at the Gavert's sign in the rearview mirror. Something about it looks familiar. I hold my hand up over part of the letters. Now I know why. **VERT'S— GAVERT'S**. *nter*—Plant Center.

We head to the corner drugstore that still has its original soda fountain. Arlo asks about my parents' farm.

"That's nice that your mom got to grow flowers and herbs. I'll bet that made her happy." I know Arlo is being polite, but it feels good that someone has asked about my parents.

At the register, I pull out my wallet, but Arlo pushes it away. "This is my treat. We can't have you broke, now, can we?"

I let Arlo pay and decide I'll put the change from the garden money in the Australia jar.

VIOLET GREETS US WHEN WE ARRIVE back at the motel. She circles the loaded-down truck and says, "Oh, my! Who's going to plant all this?"

"We are!" I say.

Ida and Horace are by the pool, but they put their wheelchairs in forward and head our way. Arlo crawls into the truck bed and hands our purchases to Roy and me. He begins to hand one to Violet, but she says, "Someone has to look after the desk."

"Afraid to get a little dirt on your hands, Violet?" Arlo asks. Violet starts toward the office and says, "I need to dress for the occasion."

Arlo laughs. "So digging in the dirt is an occasion." As she disappears, he asks me, "Am I dressed for the occasion?"

"Perfect," I say. "Except you might want to put on a tie."

A few minutes later, Violet appears in a pair of Levi's jeans and a gingham blouse that is tied at her waist. She's wearing a pair of running shoes, and her hair is pulled back in a ponytail.

"Where did you get those clothes?" I ask.

"The Lost and Found Department." She says it with

such seriousness. I should know by now Violet believes in the motto *Finders keepers.*

Violet looks adorable. And I glance over at Arlo and realize he must think the same. His face turns the color of strawberry jelly. When he realizes I've caught him studying Violet, he begins examining the hoe in his hand like it's a foreign object. He scrapes his fingernail against the sales sticker.

I stare out at the patch of ground where the garden will be. It's nothing but weeds and sparse grass, but I can see the garden. I see it thriving.

Arlo and Roy use shovels while I use the hoe to loosen the grass.

"We should have bought another hoe," Arlo says.

We pull the grass and weeds. Arlo takes off his gloves and hands them to me. I remember Dad lending me his when I was about six. Back then, I wanted to be in the garden. The next day, Dad presented me with a pair that fit perfectly. "You've officially joined the family business," he said. *Do you see me now, Dad? See? Everything you taught me about growing plants didn't go to waste. And here's what's even funnier—I like it.*

The sun has climbed high in the sky and Violet goes

back into the motel. I'm beginning to wonder if she is quitting, but then she comes out wearing a ridiculously large straw hat. I'm sure any romantic thoughts that Arlo may have had for Violet earlier will evaporate when he gets a glance of her. I must be staring too long, because Violet touches the rim and says, "This was Mother's."

Grass removal takes most of the afternoon. The sun shines bright on our little garden, and I feel pride swell inside me. And we haven't begun to plant. After breaking for late lunches on our own, we return to the garden. The whole day, my mind fights back the thought that Winston might not like the garden. That I've caused everyone to go through a lot of trouble for nothing. And what if he does get mad? Would he fire Arlo and Roy?

"The large shrubs should go in first," I say. "They'd do best here in the back."

Arlo and Roy dig the holes. Sweat drips down from their faces. They have the hard part. I add the compost. When I open the sack of worm castings, Roy grabs a big handful. "Worm castings? Sounds like a fishing category for an earthworm convention."

"Do you know what it is?" I ask him.

Roy lifts the castings to his nose and takes a big, long whiff. "Mmm. I have a feeling I'm going to know."

"Worm poop."

He drops the castings on the grass.

"Hey!" I say. "That's like gold to a gardener."

"I'll take my gold in coins."

I wish I had an apple. Whenever we planted a new tree or shrub at the farm, we sliced an apple at the site. Then we ate every bit of it except for one slice. We'd throw it into the hole before putting in the shrub or the tree. When I was little, I thought I'd see an apple tree emerge from a cedar or mesquite. But it was just a good-luck ritual my dad had thought up.

"Where do you want these?" Violet asks. She's holding the Shasta daisies.

I'm the conductor, they're the musicians, and by dusk the garden has become a symphony—or at least the start of one. Ida and Horace watch, but when it's time to water, Horace says, "We can help there."

Arlo makes a trail with heavy cardboard from the parking lot to the garden. He surrounds the perimeter with it too. That way, Horace and Ida can roll their chairs more easily.

We rest on the grass nearby while Ida holds up part of the hose and Horace waters the plants. On the left side of the garden, we rake the ground and dig up enough soil to throw down sunflower seeds. Hopefully, they will take root and bloom late in the summer.

We're quiet as we admire our work. The needlepoint hollies in the back, the knockout roses in the middle, and the dwarf mock orange in the front. Shasta daisies, phlox, agapanthus, and fountain grass surround the birdbath. It's not filled in and it doesn't yet match what I've dreamed of. But it will.

Finally, the Texas Sunrise Motel has a garden.

Chapter Twenty-One

ON OUR DRIVE BACK to Violet's house, I share my big plan. "I want to cook dinner for everyone tomorrow. We could eat outside near the pool to celebrate our garden."

"A garden party? Oh, like the scene with Sophia Loren and Cary Grant in *Houseboat*? I love parties. We could get dressed up. Can I make my strawberry lemonade cake? Everyone loves my pink lemonade cake."

I swear, it's like I've asked Alice in Wonderland to the Mad Hatter's tea.

"Thank you, Violet. I'd forgotten all about dessert."

We stop at the grocery store and I buy the ingredients for Mom's chicken enchiladas with black beans and corn.

Later I decide to make invitations. "I wish I'd bought colored pencils," I tell Violet.

"Would crayons work?"

"Sure."

She opens the butler's pantry. Inside is a big fat box of crayons and a stack of coloring books.

"I like to color sometimes," Violet says. "It relaxes me."

THE MOON IS BIG and round like a grapefruit. From bed, I watch it float between the branches of the silver maple tree. I fall asleep thinking about how pleased Winston will be when he sees the garden and how happy my parents would have been if they'd known what I did. I like to think that somehow they do.

THE NEXT MORNING, we head to the motel at dawn. Violet needs to start her shift and I need to water. I drag the long hose over to the garden.

There is something beautiful about seeing the sunrise even if it's a highway horizon. The cars are fewer, and they don't seem to zoom by like they do in the afternoon and early evening. Maybe because it's Sunday or maybe because there's a garden in the foreground. When I get to the garden, a flock of birds fly out from the holly. They scatter away so quickly, I can't tell what breed they are, only that they're gray. I remember Dad's voice. "Birds love holly because the berries provide them food and the dense branches give them shelter."

"Right again," I say aloud. Then I look back at the motel, making sure no one heard me.

No one's there.

"Right again, Dad," I whisper.

After returning the hose, I check for any weeds or grass roots we missed. Most weekends are slow at the motel. And this weekend proves that. There's only one guest car parked in the lot. I'm thinking about how a wind chime would distract from the highway roar when I hear a loud, rattling muffler.

It's Mercedes. She's not going to like that she showed up early and that the one guest hasn't vacated yet. Maybe my invitation will keep her mind off it.

She sits in the car, stretching her neck in my direction. It's as if she's sizing me up, or maybe the garden. For some reason, that makes me think about how our garden needs a bench. That way, guests could rest and enjoy the flowers. Maybe Mercedes could take a break here. A minute later, she gets out and moves slowly toward me, holding her purse straps low like the purse is heavy. She stops a few feet away from the edge of the garden and digs an orange out of her purse before dropping the bag on the grass.

I pull the invitation from my tote bag and hold it out to her. "Good morning, Mercedes! I have something for you."

She doesn't take the invitation. Instead she digs her fingernail into the orange and begins to peel. "What's that?"

"Here, open it."

"I'm eating. You open it."

I pull the invitation out and hold it up to her.

She raises her eyebrows and nods. "So?"

"It's a garden party invitation for dinner tonight."

"A garden party?"

"Nothing fancy, just dinner for everyone who lives or works at the Texas Sunrise. I hope you'll come."

"When?" She pulls at a slice of orange and pops it into her mouth.

"Around five thirty."

She chews slowly. After she swallows, she says, "I eat with my family Sunday nights."

"Oh, okay."

"I didn't say I wouldn't be here."

"Oh, great. I'm so glad you're coming."

"Maybe."

"Well, I hope maybe you can come."

She eats her orange and watches me pull a long grass runner from the ground.

"You need to add some good stuff to your dirt," she says.

"Compost?" I ask. I'd bought sacks of it and mixed it into the soil before we planted.

"Good stuff," she explains, "Eggshells, fruit peelings, orange peelings. It will make the dirt rich. Like you're in love with it."

"I did. It's called *com-post*." The way I say it sounds degrading, but I feel defensive. If there's anything I know, it's about enriching the soil.

Mercedes squats and grabs a handful of dirt. "No, this isn't so good."

Maybe she's right. Mom and Dad never bought a bag of compost. They had their own little hill at the back of the gardens by the greenhouse. They called it black gold.

When I was a little kid, I'd beg Dad to let me turn the compost pile. Then when I was eleven, it became one of my chores. Weird how being assigned to do something can take all the fun out of it. Mercedes is just trying to help.

"Would you like to plant something? There's space."

"No, no," she says, shaking her head and tearing the peelings into small pieces before tossing them into the garden. "No more gardening for me."

"Did you grow up on a farm?" I ask.

"Lots of farms. My family, we picked and picked. First we picked strawberries. Then we moved and we picked tomatoes. After that we picked beans. No, I don't pick anymore." She shakes her head. "Never."

"Well, if you change your mind, I'd be happy to include something. It doesn't have to be a fruit or a vegetable. It could be a flower."

"Or morning glories?" she asks.

"I'm going to plant some when it gets warmer. You like morning glories?"

She shrugs. "My *abuela*—my grandmother—did. She

lived in the city. Mexico City. When she was a girl, she grew them in a pot. They grew so long over the balcony, they got her in trouble."

"How's that?"

"She attached notes to the vines for a boy who lived on the first floor. She was forbidden to see this boy, but love doesn't listen to mothers and fathers. The boy would attach poems to the vine and she would pull it up to her balcony. Then she would write a letter back to him.

"My grandmother was no poet, but she could write a love letter that would cause the trees to whisper and the birds to sing all day. Because of this, everyone knew two people very close by must be in love. Her mother and father knew it wasn't them. They had never loved each other. The boy had only a mother, so they knew it was not her. The old man and woman who lived on the third floor always held hands, so people around thought, 'Ah, it must be them.'

"Then one day my abuela's mother caught one of the letters as it was being lowered. She showed her husband. He locked his daughter inside her room and dropped the pot of morning glories to the street. My abuela was so sad about the loss of the boy, the poems, the plant. All her happiness seemed to leave her with one big *ka-boom*.

"Then, later in the summer, morning glories sprouted everywhere—in the cracks in the street, up the plum tree by the curb, on the park fence across the boulevard. The wind knew the boy was her true love."

"What happened?" I asked.

"Her father decided to give the boy a chance. He unlocked my abuela's bedroom and let the boy visit in the living room. But only if her sister with the big nose could be in the same room. She had the gift of knowing what couldn't be seen.

"'The boy is boring,' she'd tell her father.

"This pleased him, and he said, 'He will make a good husband.' Her father let them marry."

"That's a wonderful story," I said.

Mercedes put up her palm. "I'm not finished. He was a good husband, but he was a poet. He was poor. When my father was born, my abuela told her husband he would have to get a job. Words could not feed a baby. They went on the circuit. Farm to farm to farm. That was their life. That was my parents' life. That was my life too. Maybe it's not such a good idea to plant morning glories. Just make sure to put in some good stuff for the dirt."

Chapter Twenty-Two

W<small>HEN A LIGHT GOES ON</small> in Horace and Ida's window, I start for their apartment. The door slowly opens a sliver. Horace is struggling on the other side. My hand goes to push, but I'm stopped, "Wait! Wait a second. I can get the door."

Horace manages to open it. Then he focuses on me and his face softens. "Stevie, good to see you. Come on in." The back of his wheelchair keeps the door open for me.

I step inside but stay near the door. I still have another invitation to deliver.

Ida is watching TV. She turns her head a little and lifts her hand in a wave.

Horace clears his throat. "I thought you might be the insurance salesman. He's supposed to be here within the hour." Boxes are stacked everywhere, mostly with things sold door-to-door or from the Home Shopping Network—Avon cosmetics and colognes, Wolfgang Puck cookware, Suzanne Somers's candy, a Kirby vacuum cleaner, and loads more. Most of the boxes haven't been opened. I wonder how they move their wheelchairs around their city of cardboard towers. Then I realize that they're stacked neatly and that wide trails run from the living room to the kitchen, bedrooms, and Horace's exercise area. Beside the parallel bars is a box marked PENSACOLA with a closed beach umbrella pointing to the ceiling.

"Sorry for the mess," Horace says.

I hand him the invitation. He reads it, looks up, and smiles. "We're invited to a dinner, lady love." Then he says to me, "We'll have to check our social calendar. Ida, how does our schedule look? If you have to, cancel that shindig with the president."

Ida giggles and pats her armrest.

Then Horace says, "We'll be there with bells on."

"Great! I'm so glad you can make it."

Ida smiles and says, "T…tank…tank you!"

"You're welcome," I tell her. "It'll be fun. See you later!" I turn the doorknob, open the door, and leave.

When the door clicks shut, I think about how it will be a long while before I take opening a door for granted.

Arlo says yes to the invitation too. "Roy isn't here, but I know he'll want to go. Hope you have plenty of food. That boy has an appetite that won't quit. I'm going broke trying to keep him fed."

As I leave, Arlo says, "Stevie, I think you're just what this old place needed."

I practically skip away. It feels like Christmas. Then a pang hits my gut so hard, I have to slow my pace. Because planning this dinner may be fun, but it's nothing like Christmas. Nothing like it at all.

THE FIRST MEAL Mom ate in Santa Fe was at Maria's. Dad ordered the tamales because Maria's was known for that (and the strong margaritas), but Mom said she was no fan of lard mixed with cornmeal. She ordered the chicken enchiladas instead. Every time she cooked them at home, she tried to make them just like the ones she'd had at Maria's, but she claimed hers never came close. I don't agree. We ate at Maria's every time we were in Santa Fe, and I thought Mom's enchiladas tasted the same. But Mom said something that made sense: "The enchiladas at

Maria's are mixed with awe." She explained that the day she arrived in New Mexico, she fell quickly under its spell. "They don't call it the Land of Enchantment for nothing," she said. Now I hope that my chicken enchiladas taste as good as hers.

I'm glad Violet suggested buying two rotisserie chickens, because the enchiladas will cook a lot quicker. And I hate to admit it, but Winston's music is kind of growing on me. A Louis Armstrong album gives just the right tempo for pulling chicken off the bone. "When the Saints Go Marching In" helps me shred the meat with a perfect rhythm. By the time Ella Fitzgerald joins him in "I've Got My Love to Keep Me Warm," I'm ready to add the cheese and put the mixture onto the flour tortillas. Rolling them is the easy part. It takes concentration to make the sour cream sauce, but I manage to do it without lumps. Mom taught me how to gradually add the flour to the butter, whisking the whole time.

After I slip the enchiladas into the oven, Violet and I push five tables, borrowed from hotel rooms, together by the garden. I'm wishing we had a couple of white tablecloths to cover them. An hour later, Violet comes to the rescue with a bolt of pink satin. "I was saving it for my future bridesmaids' dresses."

"Are you sure you want to use it? We might spill something."

"I've changed my mind about the fabric. The color seems a bit childish for a wedding."

"What will you choose instead?"

"Purple."

We unroll the yards and yards of fabric. There's more than enough to cover the long makeshift table. At Violet's urging, I let the ends flow onto the grass. The satin shimmers in the sunlight, and the forks and spoons sparkle like jewels. It's beautiful, but then I see the full picture— the murky swimming pool, the patchy land, and the highway roaring by. At the farm, sunflowers will be breaking ground right now. Soon, rosebuds will burst open. The lilacs will be showing their last blooms. Our garden is seasons away from being that lush, but it would be nice if we could hold the party in a garden like the one at home.

One day I'll return to the farm. It's what I want, and I believe it's what my parents would want too. I know that's why the farm hasn't sold. Even so, I think about calling Paco to tell him to take the sign down. The sight of Violet adding paper napkins to the place settings snaps me back. This is my today.

AT DUSK, Ida and Horace are the first to arrive. Ida wears a white eyelet dress that almost covers her Birkenstock sandals. "You look beautiful, Ida," I say.

"I told Ida she'd get another wear of that wedding gown." Horace's crisp blue shirt is buttoned up to his neck, and his hair is slicked back with a little too much gel. For the first time since meeting him, I notice his strong jawline and brown eyes. Horace is handsome. I can't believe I never realized it before.

Arlo and Roy walk up. Roy carries a bouquet of mixed flowers in a vase. He holds them out to me and says, "For your table." It's one of the sweetest bouquets I've ever seen. And the first one I've ever personally received from a guy.

"Thank you." As I take hold of the gift, my fingers brush his and a tingle runs up my arm.

"Yep, the flowers were Dad's idea." Roy stretches his arms overhead and locks his fingers together like he's relieved to be free of the task. His neck turns rosy above his white collar.

Violet had gone home earlier to change. On her return, it takes me a moment to recognize her. While she's getting out of her car, a breeze sweeps in and causes the skirt of her gauzy yellow dress to flutter like buttercup petals. She's even taken time to twist her hair into a loose bun.

For a while, we just stare at her. I glance over at Arlo, but he doesn't seem to take much notice. Then I figure maybe it's best he doesn't. When I try to picture them together, I imagine Violet pinching her nostrils at Arlo's Saturday-morning fish catch.

"You're gorgeous, Violet," I say.

Violet twirls, and the skirt lifts to her knees in the spin. "I love this dress. My aunt Mildred died in it."

We're all seated when Mercedes drives up in her gold *rat-a-tat-tat* car. She's changed out of her uniform and into a pair of snug pink capris and a crisp white shirt. Arlo is definitely noticing Mercedes as she joins us at the table.

"Sorry I was late. My mother didn't want me to leave. She said, 'You broke a commandment.' I asked her, 'What commandment says I must go to every Sunday dinner?' She said, 'The one that says you must iron me.'"

"Iron?" Horace asks, almost choking on the word.

Mercedes is trying to explain through her laughter.

"Yes, you know the commandment. Iron your mother and father?"

We all laugh. She squeezes between Horace and Roy so that she's directly across from Arlo.

I'm hoping the enchiladas aren't too spicy. My first bite proves they're not, but they're a little lukewarm. I shouldn't have brought them outside so soon. A fly buzzes around the table, and we take turns swatting it away.

Roy tucks his thumbs under his armpits and with a twang announces, "Ma'am, these here vittles are rib-sticking worthy."

"They're delicious," Arlo says.

"Yes," says Violet.

Horace wipes his mouth with the napkin. "I've had my mouth so full with this fine-tasting meal, I didn't say what I should have right off. Great job, Stevie."

Mercedes is quiet, and everyone's focused on her. When she seems to realize it, she says, "Good, Stevie. Maybe next time you can make it with verde sauce?"

"Sure. Can you can show me how?"

"I don't know how. But my mother could show you."

Horace tells us about the time he ate enchiladas near

the border. "No telling what was in them, but they were the best I'd ever had. Almost as good as these."

"Probably pigs' feet." Mercedes says it seriously, and Horace looks horrified until he realizes she's teasing.

We crack up.

Everyone makes me feel great about the enchiladas, but I could try cooking these a million times and they'd never taste as good as Mom's.

BACK AT VIOLET'S, I change into my nightgown and decide to join her in the parlor to watch Fred Astaire and Ginger Rogers, even though I don't want to. While Violet swoons at the dance numbers, I think about today. It seemed almost perfect. It would have been perfect if Mom and Dad had been there. And even Winston. After the movie, I open Mom's book and hurry to the third picture. It's an out-of-focus shot of a boy mowing the lawn. The boy reminds me of Roy—his build, the light hair—but it's blurry. He could be anyone.

Chapter Twenty-Three

It's Monday, the third day of the long weekend. And the day Winston will return. Violet and I rise early and head to the motel. The sun is hidden but casting a golden smudge between the branches along the street. Something about it makes me think of a song Dad liked, sung by Johnny Cash, "Sunday Morning Coming Down."

"Did you eat breakfast?" Violet asks in the car.

"I'll grab a Pop-Tart at the apartment."

But once we're there, I don't. Time to water the garden. Looking back at the hotel, I see Horace smoking a cigarette. He drops the butt and rolls over it with his wheelchair. Then he heads over my way. "Need help?" he asks when he notices me dragging the hose.

I almost say, "No, thanks," but then I figure Horace

can't always make that offer. So I give him the hose. The wheelchair is in the grass and I hope the ground isn't too moist. I don't want him to get stuck.

I turn the hose to a light mist, and Horace aims at the fountain grass. The sun has drifted high enough, and I can see that some weeds and grass blades have already broken ground. I squat and pull them out with gentle tugs.

"Love this time of day," he says, "when the sky shows both the moon and the sun. But I don't see the moon today."

"The moon must have run away with the North Star," I say. My mom always said that on mornings like this. Sometimes we'd hear a coyote howl. Dad would joke that it was Angelina Cruz.

"The moon must be in love," Horace says. "Reminds me of me."

"How did you and Ida meet?"

"At the hospital. I went to the war with two legs. Came back with none."

I feel awkward but resist saying sorry. I wonder which war, but I'm too embarrassed to ask. The silence between us feels heavy. Then I ask, "Ida was at the hospital?"

"Yep. She had a bad case of pneumonia. I was there getting physical therapy. She was on the upswing and had started exploring the hospital. Ida has a lot of energy. She was restless and took to wandering the floors. I was mad as a stirred hornet's nest. Bitter at what life had dealt me—my family, the government. Anything and everything made me sour. The physical therapist *really* made me want to spit fire. He was trying to get me to use my arms to cross the room on the parallel bars. I was cussing up a storm. He told me to take a break and cool off. He meant my attitude. Just then I looked across the room and saw this pretty little thing in yellow. Do you believe in love at first sight?"

I shrug. "I guess."

"Well, I didn't. Until that moment. I could see Ida's blue eyes watching me. Somehow I got a surge of strength I'd never felt and my arms walked my legless body across the room. It was a miracle." Horace flexes and points at his right biceps. "That's what love can do for you."

"Mr. Universe would be jealous," I tease.

Horace laughs. "Well, they used to be flimsy as chicken wings. They would have been after I left physical therapy, but Winston let Arlo attach some bars in our apartment. I appreciate that. Winston didn't have to do that. Didn't charge me a dime."

"Was it love at first sight for Ida?"

"Well, her mother said it wasn't."

I laugh.

"Those days, her mother talked for her. I swear that woman is the reason Ida can't speak that well. But I make her talk to me directly. I understand her just fine."

Then I ask, "Her mother didn't like you?"

Horace turns the hose away from the garden. "You're a smart kid. Crazy woman, always batting at imaginary flies. I guess it was a nervous tic or something. Nope, she still curses the day I was born. If it were up to her, I'd have never gotten past the front door. But Ida pitched a fit until her mother agreed to let me visit.

"I hired a van service to take us to the movies for our fifth date. It was the only way I could ditch her mom. The day the van pulled up, her mom grabbed her purse like she was going to chaperone. The van driver refused to let her onboard. Told her it was against the rules for able-bodied people to bum a ride. She got off in a huff and told me I'd better have Ida back before dark.

"Here's the thing. She could have gone, but I'd filled the van driver in on the witch. We became quick friends. He was more than happy to oblige. And I paid him a hundred dollars to drive us to a chapel, where we got married."

"You eloped?"

"You bet. Her mother hasn't forgiven me yet, but she writes to Ida and I write her back. Ida tells me what to say. I never write what I want to write. And I never include my name. Sometimes I feel guilty about messing up their relationship, but Ida tells me she's happy. And I choose to believe her. You ever been to Pensacola?"

"No."

"Prettiest beaches. Whitest sand. I went once when I was in the military. The navy has a big base there."

Orange spills across the sky, first a mere line, but it grows quickly.

"I've gotta get that woman to Florida. She deserves a honeymoon at the beach."

Water begins to puddle around us, and I think about how I wish I could drive. How if I could, I'd drive them to Pensacola with a big sign posted on the rear windshield that reads FLORIDA OR BUST!

Chapter Twenty-Four

VIOLET IS BUSY tidying up the office, getting ready for Winston's return.

Roy hangs out with me in the garden. We stare at the plants like we're hoping to catch something growing. But around one o'clock, Arlo takes him to Skate Land. He's on the End-of-School Party committee, and they're meeting for the final time.

When Arlo comes back, he joins me in the garden. "You mind if I plant tomatoes? We could enlarge the bed to the west and plant them along the side."

I can't help but smile. Mom mixed tomatoes and herbs with flowers in our hodgepodge potager.

"Are tomatoes funny or just the idea of me growing them?" asks Arlo.

"My mom loved tomatoes the way some people love ice cream."

"I remember."

"You knew Mom?"

"Mmm hmm." Arlo clears his throat. His face turns scarlet. "We went to school together. Before she started taking classes with Mrs. Crump."

Then he adds, "I had Roy's job and my dad was the maintenance guy. I guess you could say working for Winston is our family business. The first time he fired me was back then."

"Really?"

"I kept your mom out too late."

"You dated her?"

Arlo stares at the highway. "Oh, I guess some people call it that. We spent time together, grew up together."

Sometimes Mom teased Dad about how she should have run away with that sandy-haired boy with green eyes. It never occurred to me that the boy was real. Arlo's eyes *are* green, but his hair is brown with specks of gray. Arlo is the boy in Mom's picture.

"We weren't meant for each other," Arlo says as if he's reading my mind.

"You knew my dad?"

"Your dad came to town and your mom only had eyes for him."

"Why did he come here? Was it to work?"

"Nope. He was just passing through. I think he was going to stay one night, but he caught sight of your mom and he stayed a while."

"How long?"

Arlo studies me. "Your parents never told you any of this?"

I shake my head slightly, embarrassed to admit they didn't.

"I don't remember, Stevie. I'd better go get that shovel."

Arlo doesn't want to tell me either.

"You'll need to have some support cages," I say, then add, "I'm sorry. You probably knew that."

He turns. "As a matter of fact, I didn't. But I do now."

I hope I don't sound like a know-it-all. I have a lot to learn about gardening.

Arlo walks a few steps back. "Stevie, I know it must be hard to lose your mom. I miss her too. I miss her friendship."

"What happened to Roy's mom?" I regret the words as soon as they leave my mouth, especially when Arlo winces.

"She realized she wasn't the mothering type."

Arlo doesn't explain, and I don't ask what he means. There are some things I may never know about my parents, but this I do know: if they'd had the choice, they would never have left me.

Arlo squats and picks up some soil. "How do you reckon they gather all that worm poop?" He grins up at me, then adds, "Something you might want to know, Stevie. Your mother's garden was exactly where yours is."

Chapter Twenty-Five

I'M FILLING THE BIRDBATH in the garden when Winston turns into the parking lot. He drives slowly, stretching his neck in my direction. I've been waiting for this moment. My heartbeat picks up speed. I raise my hand to wave, but he doesn't wave back.

Winston parks the van, and it jerks back and forth before stopping. He hops out. The way he walks toward me with such purpose, I can tell Arlo predicted right. Winston is not happy about this surprise.

His lips are pulled tight into a frown. Then he asks, "What on earth possessed you to do this?"

"I thought if you just saw how much better it looks..."

"Better? Do you know how much work you just caused me?"

I examine *our* work. Until this moment, I could see the morning glory vines, the mammoth sunflowers, and pink roses in full bloom. Now I realize it was a garden in my mind. A dream. I've only planted seeds and puny perennials. Even the herbs and marigolds look silly.

"I'm sorry. I just hoped..." My voice is small.

I stand there with the hose dripping water onto my shoes.

Arlo must have seen Winston from his apartment, because he's heading toward us. "Now hold on, Winston. She wasn't the only one who did this."

Winston scowls at Arlo. "You? You were involved in this?"

"Yes." Arlo folds his arms in front of his chest. "Yes, I was."

"I'm responsible," I tell Winston. "I got him to help. Blame me."

Arlo holds his palm up to me. "Stevie, you didn't do anything wrong." Then he looks at Winston. "I could have said no, but I thought she made a lot of sense. It's not the garden, is it, Winston?"

"What are you talking about?" Winston asks.

"Memories," Arlo says. "That's what you don't like. That's what you can't face."

Winston acts like someone slapped him. His eyes turn on me a second, and then he looks back at Arlo. "If you don't like the way I run things—"

"I'm one step ahead of you. We'll be out in an hour." Arlo walks away at a quick pace.

"It's my fault," I yell. "Why can't you see what we did was good?"

Winston stares at me. This time, I look away.

Chapter Twenty-Six

HORACE AND IDA are blocking the entrance to the office. They hold signs that read NEGLECTFUL OWNER and CLEANLINESS IS NEXT TO GODLINESS. Ida's sign is attached to the back of her wheelchair and flies like a flag above her. The washing machine is broken again. I feel like holding up a sign that reads GARDEN HATER. Arlo and Roy are gone. They packed suitcases and headed out in their truck. Most of their stuff is still in their apartment, so I guess they'll come back for it. I wonder if they're staying at the Holiday Inn down the road. The garden means something different now. Arlo had warned me.

The customers going in and out of the office seem confused and curious about what's going on. One couple with matching GRAND CANYON OR BUST T-shirts are very interested in knowing the story. They hang out near the entrance, talking to Horace like they're in no hurry to see the Grand Canyon.

The lady smacks her gum and says, "You mean you've lived here for eight years and you can't wash your clothes without the washing machine breaking?"

When Mercedes finds out Arlo is gone, she crosses the parking lot and disappears into Horace and Ida's apartment. She appears five minutes later with her own sign: BAD BOSS.

The Grand Canyon T-shirt lady says, "Someone should call the television station. This should be on the news." She pulls out her phone from her yellow tote bag. "Do you want me to call them?"

Her husband, who has been quiet, now mumbles, "They don't even have cable."

A couple of businessmen squeeze around the small group to check out. When they exit the office, one of them says, "Good luck to you on the cause."

After Winston realizes Mercedes has joined the group, he comes out from behind the desk and goes outside. He hands Mercedes some money. "Here. Take Horace and

Ida's clothes when you go to the Laundromat to wash the linens."

Mercedes frowns at the money. "No, no. I'm not washing Horace's underwear."

Horace lowers his sign. "Gee, thanks."

"No offense, Horace," Mercedes says, "but that's not in my job description."

"Well, it is now," Winston says.

Mercedes grabs a marker from her dress pocket and adds MEAN.

"Mercedes, you do realize I'm your employer?" Winston asks.

"Not anymore," she says. "I quit!"

"You quit over *this*?"

Her arms spread wide and she moves them around like a conductor. "All of this. The washing machine that *ka-poot*, *ka-poot*s. You fired Arlo because of the garden."

"I didn't fire Arlo. He quit."

Mercedes is on a roll, though. "Finally something pretty to look at here, at this…this dump! And you want to poof it away. You should be happy. You have everything."

Mercedes glances at me when she says that last part. Instead of feeling good, I feel guilty. This seems like my fault—Arlo quitting, Roy quitting, now Mercedes quitting. Horace and Ida wouldn't be protesting if the garden hadn't happened.

Mercedes drops her sign and marches to her car.

"I'll wash the linens," I tell Winston, "and your clothes," I tell Horace and Ida. But Winston doesn't hear me. He just watches Mercedes drive off in her old gold Impala.

VIOLET HELPS ME CLEAN the rooms. There are only four. I want to talk about what happened, but all Violet says is "Winston is going to regret this."

Horace gives us a small pile of Ida's clothing but refuses to let us do his. "I'll wear my dirty underwear. I'm on strike."

When we drive over to the laundromat, I wonder why Violet doesn't offer to wash the clothes at her house. Then I figure she's not going to make it easy on Winston. Maybe he will cave. What would it take for Violet to quit? She probably doesn't need the money, but what would she do without her job?

While we fold the towels, Violet asks, "Would you like to come to my house for dinner?"

"When?"

"Tonight. It's a Spencer Tracy Fried Chicken party."

Of course. I like Violet's old movies. Although two people hardly make a party.

Today, Winston doesn't thank me for helping out, but he gives his approval for me to go home with Violet.

As we exit the office, Violet tells him, "I'll have her back by ten thirty p.m."

Winston doesn't object.

When we drive up, I see Arlo's truck. Roy waits on Violet's porch, leaning against one of its grand pillars.

"You found our secret hideaway," he says. "I guess we'll have to kill you now."

Dinner is fried chicken, mashed potatoes, and cole slaw. I'm thinking if Arlo couldn't fall for Violet's unique personality, maybe he could fall for her cooking skills. But when I throw away my napkin, I see the KFC cardboard bucket in the trash.

While we clean the kitchen in time for the beginning of *Adam's Rib*, I gather the courage to say the words: "Arlo, I'm sorry about your job."

"Stevie, I'll be fine." And he says it in a way that makes me believe it.

Still, I add, "I've messed everything up with my big ideas."

Arlo shakes his head. "I don't see it that way. You brought a lot of fun to our little world. For a weekend, it was nice to dream about the Texas Sunrise Motel being something more. And now a Spencer Tracy party."

"A Spencer Tracy Fried Chicken party," Violet corrects.

Arlo laughs. "Sorry. I'm just messing up everywhere." Then he winks at Violet the way Roy winks at me sometimes.

Violet blushes and I feel like I'm watching a classic movie without turning on the television.

WE'RE AT THE courtroom scene in the movie, at the part where Katharine Hepburn and Spencer Tracy drop their pencils, when Arlo's cell phone rings.

Violet hits pause, but Arlo tells us to go ahead and watch. "This could take a while."

As he walks out of the room we hear him say, "Hello, Winston."

Violet mutes the volume, and the three of us lean toward the door to listen.

"I might have to think about your offer," Arlo says. "I'll call you back."

We all straighten our posture and wait for Arlo's return. A split second later, we hear him say, "I've thought about it. I'll return under these circumstances. You buy a new washing machine. By the way, they're on sale at Sears this week. The second thing is, you keep Stevie's garden."

There's a long slice of quiet. Then Arlo says, "Why? I might want to grow a tomato or two." I love how Arlo called it *my* garden.

When Arlo enters the room, we all try to act innocent and stare at the television. "What did I miss?" he asks.

We watch Spencer Tracy's mouth moving.

Arlo smirks. "Is this a silent movie?"

Flustered, Violet hits the volume button so hard, it blares and Spencer Tracy's voice bounces against the walls.

Chapter Twenty-Seven

WINSTON NEVER MENTIONS THE GARDEN, but every morning I water it before leaving for Mrs. Crump's. And every afternoon, it's the first place I go. In just a few weeks the plants have thrived and the hollies have started to blossom. Out in the garden, I feel closest to my parents. When Winston drops me off at Mrs. Crump's house Tuesday, I notice Frida halfway down the street, walking in the direction of the square. I'm glad she's skipping. I plan to find some things out from Mrs. Crump about Mom.

This morning, Mrs. Crump says we'll stay at the kitchen table for my lessons. "Just for today," she says. "My energy has decided to take a vacation." She has dark circles under her eyes, as if she hasn't slept in days, but that would be impossible. How could a narcoleptic get insomnia? For now, I get right to the point.

"Why did Winston take Mom out of school?"

Mrs. Crump glances down at the table and wipes a crumb away. She wipes and wipes and wipes. Then she takes in a deep breath, closes her eyes, and falls asleep.

Her head bobs up and down like a float on a fishing line. Any second now, she'll let out a snore. But I've been here for long enough. It's time for some answers. When her head begins to bob again, I lift my book about Australia and drop it on the table. It lands with a loud *thump.*

Mrs. Crump's eyes widen and she blinks. "Where were we now?"

"You were telling me about Mom and why Winston took her out of school."

She's still groggy. "The baby. I told you about the baby?"

"A baby? There was a baby?"

She squirms. "Oh, dear. Dear, dear, dear, dear." She's awake now.

I scoot my chair around until it's right next to hers. "You're just telling me the truth."

She shakes her head. "This isn't my place."

"You have to be honest with me."

"He hasn't told you anything about the past?"

"He's never said a word about Mom, only that she cleaned the hotel rooms sometimes."

"Your parents never told you?"

"What baby?"

Mrs. Crump rests her hands on both sides of my cheeks and looks me square in the eyes. "Oh, dear child. The baby was you."

Everything I thought I knew runs through my head in a big wave—New Mexico, the mountains, the farm, my parents. "I was born here? In Little Esther?"

Mrs. Crump nods.

I don't remember anything about being in this town.

"Your mother never discussed what happened with me. I just knew she was with child. I thought your father was that boy who mowed the grass for the motel—I can't think of his name—but I was wrong. The last time I saw your mother was right before you were born."

"But this is such a small town."

"I lived in Japan for a few years. I was a governess there." Mrs. Crump takes a deep breath.

I don't know how to bring us back to Mom and me, so I open my Australia book and try not to wonder what else my parents lied about. But the words seem stuck to the page. There's only one thing on my mind.

"How about my dad?"

"What do you mean, dear?"

"Where was he when Mom was coming to class here?"

"I don't have an answer for that. I'm afraid you'll have to find out the rest of the story from your grandfather."

Mrs. Crump looks paler than usual, so I don't push my luck. Besides, she told me what she knows. Now I need to figure out how I can ask Winston.

Just as we're about to break for lunch, the front door creaks open. A stair squeaks and we hear someone making their way to the second floor. Mrs. Crump's eyes grow wide. I ease out of the chair, tiptoe across the room, and pick up the phone.

Just as I start to dial 9-1-1, Frida is standing in the doorway. "Here you are."

Mrs. Crump gestures to the seat next to mine. "How nice of you to join us, dear."

Frida studies both of our faces. "What did I miss?"

"You should have been here," I say. Then I hang up the phone.

Chapter Twenty-Eight

WINSTON AND I ride home in silence. The jazz station is the only sound in the van. Everything I wanted to say or ask is jumbled so tightly in my head right now that I don't know where to begin. I feel like my life has been one big lie.

Winston clicks off the radio. "Is something wrong?"

"I don't know. Is it?"

"What's that supposed to mean?"

"Nothing," I mutter. And all of a sudden I know why I can't begin to talk about it. I'm not just mad at him. I'm mad at them too.

When we get to the motel, I head out to the garden. I drop my notebooks on the ground and start pulling the weeds with my fingers. It feels good to yank something by the roots.

A few minutes later, the school bus drives into the parking lot, and after Roy steps off he waves. I wave back and he comes over to me. He throws his backpack to the side and starts recklessly pulling grass and weeds in the garden. It's really sweet that he joined me out here, but I'm afraid he's going to disturb the marigold seedlings that have barely begun to break ground.

When I stand to stretch, he peers up at me, squinting from the sun. "You wouldn't want to go to a skating party, would you?" His words come out fast and squeaky. "I mean would you want to go?"

I pause a little too long, but it's because I can't believe a guy is asking me out. Roy is asking me out.

"When is it?"

"Thursday night at seven. Dad will drive us over. It's our end-of-the-year party at Skate Land. A lot better than the Peggy and Pet City parties we had in elementary school."

"Pet City?"

"Yeah, Peggy is a clown. She'd bring goats and pigs and a donkey to the school." His voice sounds normal again. "Every year, the teachers would threaten us that they'd cancel the Peggy and Pet City party if we misbehaved. Sometimes I wanted to beg, *Please, please cancel it. What's it gonna take? Do we have to have a food fight in the cafeteria?*"

I laugh, but then I look down and realize Roy has pulled a dozen of the marigold seedlings and thrown them into the grass pile. I rescue one and hold it up in front of him.

"Roy, these aren't weeds."

"Oops." He stands and brushes off the front of his jeans. "I'm going to go see what Dad is doing. I think he may want me to build a bridge or something easier than this. Let me know about the skating party."

When I go inside the apartment, Winston is listening to jazz and reading the *Dallas Morning News*. I decide to get it over with and ask about the party but quickly change my mind. Now that I know why Mom went to Mrs. Crump, I know what Winston's answer will be.

Chapter Twenty-Nine

I TELL ROY that I can't go. It's not a full-out lie, because I don't tell him I haven't bothered to ask Winston. But it's a lie just the same. I guess I come by it naturally.

I haven't asked Winston about when I was a baby here. I'm not afraid. He should be afraid now that I know the truth. Maybe I don't want him to know that Mom and Dad never told me.

It's Thursday night, the night of the skating party, and we're eating takeout from Pete's Burgers instead of soup. The wall clock seems to click louder with each swing of the pendulum. Outside the kitchen window, I see Roy. He's wearing a white button-up shirt. Even though I wish he would, he doesn't turn and look toward our apartment.

He's sitting on the truck's bumper, staring out at the road. Arlo says, "You ready?"

"Yep."

They get in the truck and drive away.

I mix my peas into my rice.

Winston clears his throat. "I need to tell you something."

I look up.

"Paco called today."

"Paco?"

"He asked about you. I said you were doing fine. Said to tell you that you always had a home in Taos."

Winston puts his fork down and starts doing that drumming he does with his fingers.

"Did he say anything else?"

His fingers stop. "He sold the farm."

Winston blurs in front of me and I wish I could rub my eyes and he'd disappear.

"This is good news, Stevie. They paid a little more than full price because there was another potential buyer. You'll be able to go to any college you want."

I hide my face with my hands.

"Are you okay?" Winston asks.

"It was my farm. It was . . . waiting f-for me!"

Winston walks over to me and puts his hands on my shoulders. "They're not there, Stevie."

I pull away from him and head to my room. Without looking back, I say, "I hate you." I say it softly, but loud enough so that he'll hear. Then I close my bedroom door.

Inside my room, I land on my bed and bury my face in the pillow. I open my mouth, but nothing comes out. I get up, yank down the shade, change into my favorite top, and brush my hair. When I raise the shade halfway, for the first time I notice how the pull dangles at the midway point. It reminds me of one of Dad's tattoos. The rectangle with wings. Mom's escape. And tonight it's my escape too.

Outside, I tuck my hairbrush between the window and the windowsill. Horace is by the pool, smoking a cigarette. He stares at me, and I freeze. Then he looks away and blows his smoke into a zillion rings. At first I think maybe I'm mistaken. Maybe he didn't see me. But he keeps his head turned, and I realize he probably did notice. My legs move quick, hurrying away from the office to the laundry room where I get on the bike, taking off for the road that leads to town. I don't stop until I reach Skate Land.

Chapter Thirty

THE MUSIC AND THE RUMBLES of the roller skates can be heard from outside. I straddle the bike and think about turning back to the motel. But I'm tired of being a chicken. I move the kickstand into place. It's wobbly and won't hold up the bike. So I lean the bike against a tall mimosa tree, take a big breath, and go inside.

A pretty blond girl standing near Roy laughs at something he says. I almost leave.

Then he turns. A great big grin spreads across his face when he sees me, and he walks in my direction. I'm kind of torn. Happy that he's moving toward me, but I feel sorry for the girl until a guy wearing a Star Trek T-shirt hands her a soft drink. The way she looks at him, I can tell they're more than friends.

"Winston changed his mind?" Roy asks.

"I can't skate," I tell him. And that *is* true. Never have tried. Except for one failed attempt at Rollerblades around the park.

Roy leads me over to the shoe station. "What size do you wear?"

"Seven."

"Size seven," Roy tells the attendant. Then he asks me, "Where are your socks?"

I look down at my sandals and naked toes. "Oh."

Roy grins at me.

"A pair of socks, please," he tells the attendant.

The attendant pulls up a box from under the counter. I stare down at the miscellaneous used socks—polka-dotted, striped, pink, white.

"Don't worry," the guy behind the counter says, "they're clean."

I pick a white pair and resist the urge to smell them. For some reason, the whole rink smells like stinky sneaker feet.

"Follow me," Roy says. We walk to a long bench where adults, probably middle-school teachers, are watching the skaters.

Roy leads me to a spot on the bench. "Sit," he says.

I sit and wait for the next order.

"Aren't you going to take your shoes off?"

I take off my shoes.

He kneels in front of me and unlaces the skates. Then he slips one onto my right foot and pulls the laces tight. "Shut Up and Dance" begins to play. I remember the one time I tried to Rollerblade in the park. It was awkward, but I was getting the hang of it until Mom yelled, "Don't fall, Stevie." I wanted to yell "Shut up!" because hearing her say "Don't fall" somehow made me think about falling. And that's exactly what I did. Mom apologized later. "I shouldn't have said that. That's how powerful our words are."

Roy finishes lacing up the left skate. "There!" He stands easily and holds out his hands.

I just stay put.

He dangles his hands in front of me.

Finally I inhale and take hold.

He tugs, pulling me to my feet, and the move unsettles my balance. "Don't fall, Stevie!" a voice says, and it's not coming from my head.

I fall. Roy falls too. On top of me.

A few kids near us laugh.

"Way to go, Roy!" Frida stands over us, looking down. She's with a boy, and she's wearing a torn leather jacket and eyeliner.

The guy in the Star Trek T-shirt moves in. "Hey, don't trust Roy. He can't skate."

"Roy's a good guy," his girlfriend says.

Frida and her guy move away from our new circle.

We get up, Roy to his feet, me crawling to the bench. I feel like a kindergartner.

When I find my old spot, I settle there. My rear is glued to that spot. I'm making sure of it. I try not to, but I glance around searching for Frida. I don't see her.

Roy skates in a small circle, a few feet away. Then he glides up to me, holding his hands out again. "Come on. Second time's a charm."

Daya is singing "Hide Away" now. I'm not so sure about this, but I can almost hear Dad say, *Get off your rear and go for it, little girl.*

And I do.

This time I feel steady. We move toward the rink and I grab hold of the rail.

"You'll never learn like that," Roy says.

He gently coaxes me away and skates backward, leading me. The guy might not be able to tell a dandelion from a marigold, but he can skate. Slowly we begin our first round together. I've made a big deal out of nothing. I become braver on the second lap and we move a little quicker. Skating *is* fun.

"You've got good balance," Roy says.

"I was the balance beam champ of Taos Middle School's fifth-period P.E. class."

He laughs. I feel light. I could skate for hours. Then the song is over and I realize I don't know how to stop. I let go of Roy's hand and head toward the rail, letting it serve as my emergency brake. The bar hits my stomach, knocking the breath out of me.

"You okay?" Roy asks.

I nod.

"We need to work on stopping."

Roy's friends, Pretty Blond Girl and Star Trek Nerd, rush over. "You okay?" they both ask.

My face burns. This time, I'd hoped to go unnoticed.

"I'm Allie," the girl says.

"And this is Doofus," Roy says, punching Star Trek Nerd in the arm.

"I'm Adam," he says. "We know, we know. Allie and Adam, how cute."

"I'm Stevie." I smile, trying to seem confident, as confident as someone who, in less than twenty minutes, has kissed the floor twice and gotten gut punched pretty good.

"You let us know if this guy is bothering you," Adam says. And from his tone I can tell he's teasing. "I have an uncle who can make people disappear and show up in the duck pond years later."

"Oh, that won't be necessary," I tell him.

"Just let me know. I can make a phone call anytime you say."

We all laugh, and Allie and Adam skate away.

THE ROOM GROWS DARKER and the disco ball spins. Then the DJ says, "Here's a classic one for you couples only."

Stevie Nicks with Fleetwood Mac sings, *I took my love and I took it down. Climbed a mountain and I turned around.*

Roy grabs my hand. "Come on."

"Landslide." Mom and Dad's song, the one they both loved. I feel a pull at my heart and remember them dancing outside under the cottonwood tree. I must have been five. I'd crawled out of bed and peeked between the drapes in my bedroom. The night was clear and the stars filled it like someone had tossed them across a blue velvet sky. I watched for a while. Then I crawled back into bed and fell asleep.

Our fingers are locked and I can't tell if it's my sweat or his that makes my hands feel slippery. All I know is that I'm thankful Roy is guiding me around the floor. Everyone looks blurry—the couples skating by, the flecks of flashing light from the disco ball above us. That song makes all of this seem like a dream.

When the song ends, I tell Roy, "I'd better leave."

"The party isn't over."

"I—I have to leave."

Roy tilts his head to the side and examines my face. "Winston doesn't know you're here, does he?"

"What do you think?"

He stands there, not saying anything.

I skate over to the rail.

"Hold on. You're going to walk by yourself in the dark?"

"I rode Violet's bike."

Roy smirks. "I heard the pink thing was yours."

"Whatever."

I'm taking off my skates and Roy sits down next to me and removes his too.

"You don't have to quit."

"I asked you here, didn't I?"

My face feels warm all over. I guess this is my first date.

We walk outside and I turn to the right, where I left the bike leaning against a tree.

"Where's the bike?" Roy asks.

I walk over to the empty spot. "It was here."

"Well, it's not here now."

"I see that," I snap.

"Maybe you forgot. My dad forgets where he parks the truck all the time."

"I didn't forget. It was here." Until this very moment, I didn't want that bike, and now all I can think of is how excited Violet was when she gave it to me. How disappointed she's going to be when she knows I lost it.

While I stare at the spot, Roy walks a wide circle around Skate Land.

"Hate to break it to you, but it looks like your bike is gone."

When I don't say anything, Roy says, "Don't worry. It was just an old bike. It was too little for you anyway."

"It was a gift. It was Violet's. This has been a really bad day."

"Did something else happen?" Roy asks.

I almost tell him about the farm and what I learned about Mom, but I change my mind and say, "I need to get home."

"Wait here a second." Roy goes inside and then comes right back. "We've got a ride."

He reads the panic on my face and adds, "I promise, we'll be home soon."

A FEW MINUTES LATER, we crowd into Adam's big brother Link's car. Roy and I have to sit so close, our arms and legs touch. In the car, the guys joke about some stupid movie they've seen, but all I can think about is the bike.

How am I going to tell Violet? And as much as I don't want to blame Frida, I can't help but think she had something to do with this. After all, she had disappeared after the big fall.

When we get about a quarter of a mile from the motel, Roy says, "Let us out here. We'll walk the rest of the way."

"Moonlight walk, huh?" Adam teases.

"Good night, jerk," Roy says. Then to Link, "Thanks for the ride."

"Yes, thank you," I say. "Nice to meet you."

"Maybe we can go shopping sometime," Allie says.

"I'd like that," I tell her.

Roy and I walk in silence, letting the crickets' concert fill the air.

I'm still thinking about my parents and their dance below the stars.

"You know, Stevie, Winston really isn't that bad."

"I didn't say he was."

"He just seems sad to me," Roy says.

When we reach the garden, Roy and I stop and stare at the ground.

"Well, it's still here," Roy whispers.

"Yep, it sure is."

We're standing beneath the Texas Sunrise Motel sign. The VACANCY sign flashes, turning us red every other second. Roy picks up my hand and kisses it. It's a small kiss, a peck really, but I've never been kissed before, and I'm counting this one. Then he steps toward me and his lips touch mine for a long moment. At least long enough for the sign to flash six times.

"Good night," I whisper, and take off, hearing him call out to me in a hushed voice, "Good night, Stevie!"

I move briskly toward my bedroom window. I'm relieved to see the hairbrush in the same place I left it. I lift the window and step inside. My foot lands on an object, probably one of my shoes, and I fall to the floor, my third fall this evening, but at least I'm back in my room.

Then I hear, "Like mother, like daughter."

Winston sits in a chair a few feet from my window. Before I can stand, he gets out of the chair and leaves.

I stretch out on the bed, fully dressed, and wait for Winston's snoring. It takes a long time tonight. So long that I fall into a light slumber. At four thirty, I wake up and ease out of bed. Winston doesn't usually get up until five, so I make good use of the time. I throw a few things into my backpack—underwear and tops. The record player and the stack of records beckon to me. They'll have to stay. Then I open the window and slip out, not bothering to close it.

Like mother, like daughter, I make my escape. I head in the direction of the highway. I don't look over my shoulder. Except for a sliver of moon, it's pitch dark. With the motel at my back, I walk in the grass along the service road, trying to get my bearings. When I do, I turn and face west. I'll go home. I'll tell Paco to stop the sale. That it's my farm.

I take a few steps, then stop.

I plop down on the grass and hit my fists against the ground, over and over again.

Chapter Thirty-One

MY BEDROOM WINDOW is down and locked. I've been caught again. This time I don't care. The drapes from the office are closed, but the lamp from inside casts an orange glow on them.

I head toward the office door and slowly open it, causing the warning alarm to hold its buzz longer than usual.

"Checking out?" Winston asks.

At first I think he doesn't know it's me. Then I realize he does.

"No," I whisper.

I wait for him to say something. Anything. Checkmate. You win. But Winston's eyes are soft. It's like he's concerned but doesn't know what to say. So I say it for him.

"Good night."

"Good morning," Winston says back.

I go to my room and go to sleep, counting the years I have before I can take off for Australia.

THE ALARM CLOCK IS UNDER MY PILLOW, and its dull ringing wakes me up. I must have covered it when it went off earlier. It's fifteen minutes past the time I usually get up, so I quickly get dressed and don't bother to eat. "I'm ready," I tell Winston.

He grabs his keys and turns the BE BACK SOON sign around. "Let's go."

As we move away from the apartment he says, "How about dinner out tonight?"

TODAY IS THE LAST DAY of class. I almost forget, until I see Frida get off the back of her mom's motorcycle with a Tupperware container.

Before taking off, her mom hollers, "Save me a cupcake!"

I was supposed to bring something too. I'd even thought of making cookies.

"Did you learn to skate?" Frida is smiling a little. I figure she's gloating about how she got away with stealing my bike. Violet's bike.

"Where'd you go off to with your boyfriend?" I ask.

"Stub? He's not my boyfriend. Our mom and dad go out together. He's like a brother."

"Whatever," I mutter.

"What'd you say?"

Mrs. Crump opens the door. She's wearing a red straw hat and a purple pantsuit. A spicy tomato smell fills the house.

"There're my students. Ready for your party?"

"Mrs. Crump, that hat is rockin'. Going anywhere special?" Frida is acting strange with this phony politeness. Even her voice sounds gooey.

Touching the brim, Mrs. Crump says, "I'm a member of the Red Hat Society. We're having a lasagna luncheon here right after class."

I forgot to tell Winston we get out early today. He probably doesn't even realize it's the last day. I ask Mrs. Crump if I can use her phone in the kitchen. While she and Frida go upstairs, I leave a message for Winston at the motel.

Frida is sitting diagonally across from Mrs. Crump at the table. There are chips and dip on the table, and the two of them have already started attacking the food. They look as cozy as Violet and me in her parlor with our bowl of popcorn.

"Frida was just telling me she saw you at the skating rink last night."

I glare at Frida so hard, she squirms. She looks confused.

"I didn't know how to skate, but I did a few laps before the end of the night. Of course, Frida probably didn't notice that."

"No," Frida says, "I had to leave early."

"I wanted to leave early too, but someone stole my transportation." I stare right at her. She's not getting off the hook so easy.

Frida frowns and opens up the container. There are six cupcakes with light-brown frosting.

"That's dreadful," Mrs. Crump says to me. "Did you get it back?"

"No." I keep my eyes on Frida.

"How about a cupcake?" Frida holds out the container to Mrs. Crump.

Mrs. Crump leans over the goods and smiles. "Chocolate?"

"German chocolate," Frida says proudly. "I made them."

Mrs. Crump grabs one. "German chocolate is one of my favorites, and I haven't had it in ages."

Frida turns the container to me, but I shake my head and grab a chip.

Mrs. Crump nibbles at hers. "Scrumptious, Frida! And you made them yourself. I'm impressed. You're so creative."

"She's creative all right," I say.

Frida narrows her eyes at me and grabs one of the cupcakes before sealing the container top back on.

Two folders are underneath the atlas. I recognize one—my Australia report. Mrs. Crump hands Frida hers. "I learned so much about Pluto from your report."

Pluto isn't even a planet. And it certainly isn't studied in other geography classes.

Frida peeks at the grade. She looks pleased, so it must be good.

Roy is right. Mrs. Crump is a joke of a teacher.

She gives me mine. "You are a writer, Stevie."

I guess Mrs. Crump isn't that bad.

"I can tell you want to go to Australia, the way you wrote about it," she says.

I think of my jar. Right now, Australia seems as impossible as the farm.

"What do you girls have planned for the summer?" Mrs. Crump asks.

"I'm going to my dad's," Frida says. "He lives in San Diego."

They both turn their heads to me.

"I'm taking care of a garden," I tell them.

"What have you planted?" Mrs. Crump glances at the clock. I guess she's thinking about the grand ol' time she's going to have with those Red Hats.

Somehow we manage to eat and chat about nothing for two hours. Frida tells me her mother likes to garden. I do my best not to act impressed, but I'm trying to imagine her mom planting and pruning wearing her tight leather pants.

Mrs. Crump checks the clock again, then says, "I look forward to seeing you next year."

"I won't be back next year." Frida seems thrilled about this announcement.

"Oh?" Mrs. Crump asks, but she doesn't sound surprised or disappointed.

"My mom was going to call you soon. I'm going to the high school."

Right now I feel like I've been sentenced to four years of solitary confinement. And I'm not even the criminal.

We make our way downstairs just as the doorbell rings. A red and purple wave can be seen through the front door's glass. Mrs. Crump's Red Hat Society has arrived. Then Frida does something that makes my jaw drop. She turns and gives Mrs. Crump a big hug. "You're a cool lady," she says.

The way Mrs. Crump's eyes light up, I can tell she likes hearing that.

Then Frida whispers in her ear, but I hear her anyway. "Thanks for passing me."

She skips most days and still passes? What a scam.

Mrs. Crump hugs me. "See you in September, Stevie."

The Red Hat ladies buzz in, laughing and talking with one another, bringing a powdery floral scent into the foyer. They hardly notice Frida and me as we leave. No sign of Winston. Frida heads toward her mom, who's at the curb, straddling her motorcycle, smoking a cigarette.

Frida stops and turns. "By the way, I didn't steal your bike." She sounds sad and disappointed.

She puts on her helmet, hops on the back of the motorcycle, and leans into her mom's right shoulder. They take off, with Frida holding tightly to her Tupperware container. The motorcycle roars down the block, Frida's mom's hair blowing wildly. And even though Frida didn't give me any reason at all to believe her about the bike, for some reason now I do.

Chapter Thirty-Two

WINSTON'S VAN IS IN SIGHT. I want to get out of here. I want to go to my room, lock the door, and stay inside forever. But before I do, I have to tell Violet about her bike.

When I buckle my seat belt, Winston asks, "Did you eat too much party junk to have lunch? I thought we'd go out now instead of supper."

"Sure."

"How was the last day?" He sounds interested. And now I don't feel like talking. At least about school.

"It was fine." Then I add, "Frida won't be there next year."

"Is she moving?" He sounds almost happy at the thought of it.

"No. She's going to the high school."

"I see."

"Not me, though. Right?"

Winston changes the subject. "I think you'll like the menu here. It's the place with the cupcakes."

We drive around the courthouse, then past the Confederate soldier statue, and make our way to the Rise and Shine Diner.

Winston orders the breakfast special—three eggs, bacon, hash-brown potatoes, and Texas toast. I order a green-chili hamburger and potato salad. He surveys the restaurant and nods to a man across the room.

The man nods back. Since I've been here, I've learned that's a Texas greeting of sorts. A two-old-men-who-kind-of-know-each-other greeting.

Winston and I don't talk. We just take in the diner's sounds, the clinks of the plates against silverware, and bits of other people's conversations.

When our meals arrive, Winston breaks the silence. "You have an aunt who'd like to see you."

My entire body goes numb. "Mom had a sister?"

He shakes his head and wipes away the egg yolk on his lips. "Your dad. *His* sister."

"Why didn't—" I don't finish the question, because I realize it wasn't his place to tell me.

Winston picks up on my unfinished question. "I didn't know about her or I'd have told you sooner. She just learned about you."

That means she just found out about Dad and Mom's accident. "She called you?"

"Yes. She found me. Not sure how. Probably Paco. But, anyway, she lives in Louisiana. Has some plant business, a nursery. She'd like you to visit."

I don't know what to think. This is like saying some stranger has a right to know me suddenly. She must not be that great if Dad never told me about her.

"I had her checked out," Winston says. "She seems like a decent person. I think it's a good idea for you to go there."

He doesn't say for good or a week or a weekend.

"What's her name?"

"Teresa Smith."

"Smith? Are you sure she's a real person?"

"Yes," he says. "She's excited to meet you. Said her children are too. She says you can come next week."

"What if I don't want to go?"

"You don't seem happy here. I think you should meet your family."

Something is building inside me and I can't hold back. I won't hold back. Not this time.

"I know I was born here," I blurt a little too loud. A few people turn their heads in our direction.

Winston inhales long and hard. I expect he's going to ask me how I know, but instead he says, "I should have told you. I guess I thought your parents would have."

"I'd ask them, but they're not here anymore."

He pushes his plate away even though there're still two pieces of bacon drowning in yolk. "What do you want to know?"

"Everything."

The waitress comes by to ask if we're ready for our check. "We're going to be a while," Winston tells her. "Coffee?" he asks me.

I nod.

We wait until the coffee arrives before we start. I put a lot of sugar in mine. So much so that Winston says, "You don't have diabetes, do you?"

"Not unless you can get it from eating a whole bunch of canned soup."

Winston smiles at that, but I don't want to get too comfortable. I feel like my past was one big lie. I need the truth.

Winston glances around the diner and leans toward me, speaking in a lower voice. "Look, it was messy. Your dad didn't know your mom was expecting you. I made Sheppard leave. I even gave him my motorcycle. He'd admired it and I figured it would get him away from her quicker."

I should have known. Dad wouldn't have deserted Mom. I don't tell Winston we still had the motorcycle until Paco sold it with all the other stuff. Now it makes sense that Dad snapped at me when I asked why he never rode it. Maybe that's why he never sold it either. He didn't think it was his to sell.

"How long was he here?"

"Two weeks. Three. Maybe a month." Winston squirms in his seat. "Listen, I don't remember. Your mom was still seventeen. He was too old for her."

After Mrs. Crump opened up I'd done the math. "She was almost eighteen and he was only twenty."

I remember Dad's words. His only words about Winston. *He didn't like the likes of me.*

His tattoo with the daisy and tornado flash into my thoughts. Mom's tornado is sitting across from me. And now I'm caught up in the same storm.

Out the window, people are passing by. I search each face. Did they know me? Did I know them? "But all I remember is New Mexico."

I take a swig of coffee.

"Your dad came back when your mom turned twenty. You were two." His voice cracks on those last words, and he looks away toward the bathroom.

We move our silverware around our plates, but we don't eat anymore. It's just the scratching of the forks filling the space.

Then Winston says, "Look, go see your aunt. Ask her questions about your dad. She may know the answers I can't give you."

I want to say, *But* you *haven't answered all of them.* I can tell he's finished by the way he holds up his hand to flag down the waitress for the check.

I thought his telling me more about what happened

would answer everything. But it's like he's given me a jigsaw puzzle with pieces missing.

He stands, as if he's saying, *This is finished.*

"When did my grandmother die?" I ask him.

Winston sits back down. I think this is the one question he didn't want to answer. "Was it when we were in New Mexico?"

Winston stares out the window again and shakes his head. "The year before your dad showed up the first time."

He's still shaking his head when the check arrives.

Chapter Thirty-Three

ON THE DRIVE BACK to the motel, my head is full of what Winston said. I was two when I left Texas for New Mexico. Even though it's only a couple of years, it feels like I've been robbed of something. Memories. Mom documented everything. It was important to her. Why not this?

My mind drifts to Louisiana. I always knew Dad was from there, but I thought there wasn't any family left. If only I'd known that being a good kid, trying never to ask my parents questions that I thought would hurt them, would end up hurting me.

When we approach the motel, I see something dangling from the sign. A bicycle. Not my bicycle, but a fancy adult-size one with a chain threaded through the spokes.

Winston slows the car and lets it creep up for a closer look. "What the ...?"

Whoever played this cruel prank trampled the garden to do it. The shrubs and perennials are uprooted and there are muddy footsteps in the soil where I planted seeds and where seedlings had started to sprout.

This has been a lousy day, and it's not over yet.

Winston doesn't get mad like I thought he would, like I wish he would. I want someone to scream. All the work, all the hope I had for the garden, gone for a silly prank.

Violet is in the office stacking invoices. "Did you see?"

Winston says, "Yep. Have you called the police?"

"Not yet. Do you think we should?"

Winston stares at her.

"I'll call the police." Violet picks up the phone.

I step forward. "Just a second, Violet."

She pauses.

I stare out the window. A man is cleaning the swimming pool. I take a deep breath and say, "Your bike was stolen too. I'm so sorry. I shouldn't have ridden it to ..."

I'm having trouble saying "Skate Land." It makes me think of too much bad that happened.

Violet doesn't bat an eyelash. She dials the number

and tells an officer about the bike hanging from the sign and the pink princessmobile being stolen. She's on the phone quite a while, listening.

"I see. Really? Well, that is strange. Thank you, Officer Halbert." She hangs up.

Winston and I are waiting for her to say something.

"Well?" Winston asks.

"This is a peculiar day. Seems bikes have been stolen all around Little Esther and they're being found hanging from trees and signs."

"Did they demolish any other gardens?" I ask.

"What?" Violet asks.

My words come out shaky. "Somebody—I guess the person or persons who hung the bike—destroyed everything in the garden."

"Everything?" At least Violet seems to care.

I try not to look out the window, but I look anyway.

Violet scoots her chair away from the desk, stands, and puts her arm around me. "You know what you need?"

When I don't say anything, she says, "Debbie Reynolds and Gene Kelly."

"What?"

"*Singin' in the Rain.* Have you ever seen it?"

"No." She means well, but I'm a little annoyed that she thinks old movies are the answer to everything.

The office door opens, and Roy enters. His face is flushed, like he's been running. "You've got to see this!"

"We have," Winston says. "It's being taking care of."

Roy studies me. Violet still has her arm around me. "What's wrong?" Roy asks.

I want to ask, *Didn't you notice the garden?* But I know that it's not the only thing killing me inside. I slip out of Violet's hold and walk toward the apartment door. When I touch the knob, I turn. They're all staring at me.

I ask Winston, "Can I go see my aunt next week?"

Chapter Thirty-Four

THIRTY-SEVEN BIKES were reported missing, and thirty-eight have been found. It's been the talk of Little Esther.

"I wonder where they got the extra one," Roy says.

"This is like a Nancy Drew mystery," Violet says. "The title could be *The Mystery of One Found Bicycle*."

Officer Halbert told Violet that we might have to wait until the end of the week to get the bike. The city couldn't quite figure out who was responsible for gathering the bikes and returning them to their owners. The police department said the fire department should have to do it, and the fire department said they had more important things to do than rescue kittens and pull bikes out of trees and off signs. We still didn't know where the Pink Princess was.

Arlo, Roy, and I decide to take a ride around town to see the hanging bicycles. Maybe we'll find Violet's. After a few miles, we spot our first, in a crepe myrtle in front of Julio's, a Mexican and Italian restaurant about a mile off the square. It's not the pink princessmobile, though.

Mrs. Crump's next-door neighbor has one dangling in the shade of a giant oak tree. A crowd is gathered around it, staring up, and some people take pictures. We park and get out of the truck to ask if anybody knows where other bikes are.

"There's one at the end of Third Avenue, in front of the yellow house," a boy on a bike tells us.

"Looks like you lucked out," Arlo tells him.

"Huh?"

"No one took your bike."

The boy leans on his handlebars. "Nah, but I sure wish they had. That would have been awesome."

"Why would you think that?" Arlo asks.

"You'd get it back. And your bike would have had an adventure."

One lady shows us a list she's made from all the sightings. "I think it's art," she says. She drove all the way from North Dallas to see them.

We thank the lady but decide it's more fun discovering them on our own.

Back in the truck, Arlo says, "Crazy lady. Art? Give me a break."

Roy laughs. "She's from Dallas. What do you expect?"

After seventeen bike discoveries, none being Violet's, we decide to go back. It's getting dark, anyway.

Roy has been kind of quiet, but now he asks, "Are you going to live with your aunt?"

"I don't even know her." And I don't know why she wants to know me now. Hasn't she had years to find out about me?

I wake up to the sounds of kids laughing and splashing. It's Memorial Day weekend. The pool is finally open.

AT BREAKFAST, Winston shoves the *Dallas Morning News* across to me. The headline reads LITTLE ESTHER BIKE MYSTERY, ART OR CRIME? There's a picture on page two of a bike hanging from a tree. There are a lot of people gathered around it, but I can see Skate Land in the background. I look closely at the picture. There's a banana seat and a little bell on the handlebars, next to a basket. It's my bike. I mean Violet's. It was there at Skate Land the whole time.

"But we looked around Skate Land. *All* around it."

"Did you look up?" Winston asks.

"We didn't look up."

He chuckles.

I'm feeling relieved. I shake my head and laugh a little. I keep thinking about what that boy said, how your bike could go on an adventure. I'd rather be on the adventure myself. That's how I've decided to look at the visit with my aunt. An adventure. Like it or not, something is bound to happen.

Chapter Thirty-Five

WINSTON BUYS A TICKET for me to Alexandria, Louisiana. He says my aunt Teresa has a plant nursery in a small town called Forest Hill. I leave tomorrow, but first I need to do something important. I need to let Frida know how sorry I am that I thought she took my bike. Violet's bike. Four university students admitted to the prank. Their entire fraternity was suspended for a semester, but they probably got a lot of slaps on the back from admirers. It gave people around here something to talk about for a few days. In my opinion, that's more interesting than hearing everyone talk about when they think it might rain.

When I ask Roy if he knows where Frida lives, he

tells me she lives about five miles away on the other side of town in a little green house.

He's been acting funny ever since Skate Land. Maybe he wishes he hadn't asked me. Maybe he wishes he hadn't kissed me too.

Then he says, "If you want, I'll go with you."

I'm relieved and grateful.

I think about saying yes, but instead I say, "This is something I need to do by myself."

The garden is in shambles, but I notice the blooms on the white rosebush, the only thing that might have a chance if someone waters it. That won't be me. I'll be in Louisiana, and even if I wasn't, I don't know if I have it in me to rebuild the garden. What use is it to make something beautiful if someone's going to come along and destroy it?

I cut a few of the roses and find some green tissue paper in the supply closet. Violet says it's left over from Christmas decorations. I twist the tissue paper around the stems and secure it with some twine the way I saw Mom do a million times for customers.

Then I put the bouquet in the bike's basket, hop on

the seat, and pedal to the little green house on the other side of town.

Frida's neighborhood is nothing like Mrs. Crump's and Violet's. The houses are small and the yards are closer together. But there are people mowing their lawns and kids running through a sprinkler system. A green house is at the end of a cul-de-sac. There's no lawn. Instead, half a dozen raised beds with vegetables fill the front yard. A huge rosemary plant grows next to the front door. The garage door is open, and Mrs. James's motorcycle is parked next to a long table with a bunch of stained glass on one end. The piles are organized by colors—purple blue, and red.

I start toward the front door when I realize Mrs. James is at the back of the garage. I'd recognize that long braid and the leather pants anywhere.

"Mrs. James?"

She turns. She's wearing gloves and safety glasses.

"Yeah?"

"Mrs. James, I'm Stevie, Frida's . . . classmate."

She pushes the glasses up so that they are resting atop her head. A pair of pliers is in her hand. "Oh, yeah.

I've seen you. You're the girl with the pink bike." I wonder if she knows I accused Frida of stealing it.

"Is Frida here?"

"She's in San Diego."

"Oh, well, I guess I'll wait until she gets back."

"That might be a while. Frida called last night and said she's staying there for good." Mrs. James says this in a matter-of-fact tone.

"Oh." I'm wishing I could think of something else to say. The overhead light reflects against a piece of emerald-green glass on the table.

"She'll be back," Mrs. James says. "This isn't the first time. She thinks her dad created the planet, but she'll see what it's like now that he has a new wife and kid."

I don't say "oh" again. I just stay quiet.

"Are the flowers for her?"

I look down at the roses. They look kind of pitiful compared with Mrs. James's garden. "Yes, they were, but you can have them."

She walks over and takes the roses from me. She gives them a long whiff. "Mmm, Autumn Delight. Love old-fashioned roses. Thanks, Stevie."

Now that she's stepped away from the table, I can see

the entire piece that she's working on. Yellow roses with ivy loop around the edges. "That's beautiful. Do you do a lot of stained glass?"

She lightly strokes the piece with one finger. "It's my job."

"You're an artist, Mrs. James."

She shrugs. "I try. Frida's an artist too. You should see the amazing job she did on my friend Hal's porch. Holy moly, what she can do with a can of spray paint."

My face burns remembering the day I thought I caught Frida doing graffiti. I guess I read her all wrong. Except for the skipping. She's as guilty as Carmen when it comes to that.

Mrs. James interrupts my thoughts. "You be looking for Frida to come back. She won't stay long in San Diego. Mark my word."

I turn to leave, then turn back again. "Mrs. James, did you know my mom?"

"I knew her. She was Winston Himmel's daughter, and for a while everyone knew Winston."

"Because of the motel?" I ask.

She pulls off the goggles and says, "Because of the motel? Stevie, your grandfather was one of the best jazz musicians in Texas. It's not my kind of music, but my parents loved his band. So did a lot of people."

"What instrument did he play?"

"He played everything, but he was known for the piano. Your mom never told you about his band?"

I barely shake my head.

She presses her lips together, then says, "Well, he stopped playing after his wife died. At least, that's what I heard. Your grandmother was a nice lady. I used to see her at the diner a lot. She always spoke to me. Not everyone in this town is friendly to people who ride motorcycles. They treat us like we're in the Hell's Angels.

"Your mom was a little younger than me, but I remember sometimes seeing her walking around town, carrying you on her hip like a little monkey. She always looked sad. But I could tell she was crazy about you."

"Well, I guess I'd better be going. When you talk to Frida, tell her I said hello." Then I ask, "Can I have her mailing address? There's something I have to tell her."

"Of course." Mrs. James jots down the address on a notepad from a drawer and hands it to me.

When I turn to leave, Mrs. James says, "Stevie, don't

hold it against your mom for not telling you about your granddad. She must have had her reasons."

Yeah, I'm thinking. He was cold and he was tough on her.

Then Mrs. James says, "Maybe she missed him but she didn't know how to come back. Now Frida, she knows how to come back. And this door will always be open for her."

Chapter Thirty-Six

SINCE I'M LEAVING TOMORROW, I make dinner tonight. I have time because it took only fifteen minutes for me to pack. I don't even know how long I'll be gone. Winston said for me to decide after I've been there a few days and he'll buy a return ticket for me. He'll send it to my aunt. I'm not sure what to think about that. Does he want me to stay all summer?

I decide to make chicken-fried steak again since Winston liked it so much. Before I begin cooking, I go through Winston's record stash, but I don't see any covers that look like Winston or any that have his name anywhere. If Winston stopped playing after my grandmother died, maybe he got rid of his recordings.

I take time on the potatoes, mashing them to a

smooth, creamy pile. I make extra gravy because I noticed how Winston ate every drop last time. Since I'm through cooking before Winston comes in from the office, I wash the pots and pans.

From the kitchen window, I see Horace and Ida sitting out by the pool. They are dark silhouettes against the setting sun. They're watching a dad teach his little girl how to float on her back. Dad showed me how to do that at Eagle Nest Lake. I must have been about three or four. I squeeze my eyes shut and try to remember before then. When I was here, in this very apartment. I look around the room, searching for something familiar. This was my first home and I don't remember anything about it.

Winston interrupts my thoughts. "Dinner smells wonderful." He sounds cheerful. Maybe because he's getting rid of me for a while.

"Thank you."

When we sit at the table he says, "You shouldn't have gone to this trouble."

I shrug. "We have to eat."

"There's always soup." He's smiling.

I don't know why, but right here at the table, I break down.

Winston looks helpless. He was just about to take his first bite and I've ruined it. I put my napkin to my face, but I'm not hiding anything.

His chair scrapes against the floor and I figure he's going to leave me alone, let me get myself under control. But then I feel a hand on my right shoulder. Then my left. "I know." There's that crack in his voice again. The one I heard when he talked about Mom leaving.

I drop the napkin and ask, "Why didn't you ever visit us?"

Winston lets go of my shoulders. "We said things... things that couldn't be taken back."

I push my chair away from the table and stand. "Then you were all stupid."

Winston nods. "You're right. The three biggest fools that ever lived."

For a long moment, we're silent, staring at our untouched meals. Then I clear my throat and say, "Mrs. James said you played the piano in a band."

His head jerks a little. "She did, huh? I'm surprised she would know that. I doubt we played her kind of music."

"She knows more about you than I do. Everyone does."

Winston gazes out the window. Then suddenly he stands and says, "Come on."

"What?"

"Let's go for a ride."

"Our supper…"

"Just cover it with Saran Wrap." He looks down at my bare feet. "Then put on your shoes and meet me in the van."

A few minutes later, I'm walking outside wearing my flip-flops. Winston has hung the BE BACK SOON sign on the door.

I buckle up and ask, "Where are we going?"

"Be patient," he says, but I can tell he's not mad.

We drive across town to the Little Esther General Hospital, a one-story building that faces the highway. "Stevie Grace, this is where your life began. Your mom"—he stops and swallows—"your mom woke me up and said, 'My water broke.'

"I ran three red lights. I was afraid I would have to deliver you."

I'm wondering about Dad when Winston points to

the building. "You were born in that corner room. I think. Maybe it was next to the corner room. You only spent a day there. Or maybe two. I don't remember. I do remember I couldn't for the life of me figure out why she'd named you Stevie. I had a problem with that until she said your middle name would be Grace."

"That was my grandmother's middle name."

He gives me a look that says, *How would you know that?* Then he answers, "Yes, that's right."

"Did Dad ever try to get in touch with Mom after he left?"

"Yes, for a while, but I threatened to have him arrested if he tried to contact her again."

The air feels thick in the van, and I push the window button so that I can breathe. "Why didn't you call Dad and tell him about me?"

Winston shakes his head. "Stevie, when you reach my age, you'll have had a long time to think about things you've done over the years. You'll twist them every which way in your head, play them out like a bad song you can't shake."

I'm mad at Winston, but I'm also tired of being mad

at him. It's hard to be angry with someone when they admit they're wrong.

He pulls out of the parking lot, drives to the square, and stops at the Rise and Shine Diner, not bothering to cut the engine. He stares at the diner for so long, I'm starting to think something's wrong. Finally he says, "Your mom used to come here with you every Saturday morning and eat pancakes. She fed you your baby food until you got old enough to eat pancakes too."

"Did you come also?"

"No, but I knew she was here because I followed her one day. Eventually, I got up enough nerve to ask if I could join the two of you, and she said, 'Maybe, but not now.' For a while, I figured she just wanted to be alone with you. It was your special time together. But I think it was something else."

He pauses so long that I think he's not going to tell me. "Why?" I ask.

"I think she came here with your dad." The way Winston says that makes me think he's just realizing why himself. He puts the car in reverse and heads away from the square.

At the H-E-B grocery store, he points to a spot that has a water machine. "There used to be a toy pony there. The kind where you put quarters into a slot and ride. You loved it. You'd hold one arm up and say, 'Giddyup, horsey, giddyup!'" He laughs a little.

When we pass the post office, he tells me how he'd let me pick out the postage stamps, and then he takes me by a park and says, "You loved to swing but hated the merry-go-round. It made you sick."

That gives me goose bumps, because I once got sick on the Tilt-A-Whirl at a carnival in the park. Ever since then, I can't stand to spin.

By the time we reach the motel, Winston points to the garden, now in shambles. "Before you were born, your mom planted a garden there. Even after you were born, she'd get out there and work in it. She'd put a little quilt on the ground and you'd sit there and pull up the clover."

"What happened to the garden?"

"A garden needs someone to take care of it."

For a second, I wonder about the farm. What will happen to the garden there? Will the new owners take care of it?

When Winston parks, he turns to me and says, "Stevie, this was your first home."

I stare at the motel office door. The BLOOMIN' OFFICE sign hangs right by the BE BACK SOON one. To the left is the set of apartment windows—the kitchen, Winston's room, and mine, the one that Dad had tattooed on his arm, the exit Mom and I failed to escape from.

He pulls the keys out of the ignition. "Are you hungry?"

"Starved," I tell him.

Winston takes down the BE BACK SOON sign.

"What did I call you?" I ask. An hour ago I didn't want to know, but somehow the tour of my life has made me curious.

He lets out a little snort. "Winnie."

Chapter Thirty-Seven

VIOLET TAKES THE MORNING SHIFT so that Winston can drive me to the bus station in Dallas. She gives me a DVD with a pink bow on top—*Singin' in the Rain*. "Just in case you need it."

"Thanks, Violet."

Then she hugs me. "When you return, we'll have another girls' beauty night." She slips back behind the desk.

Outside, Roy and Arlo show up just as Winston starts the engine. "I have good timing," Roy says. "I got out of loading the van."

"There's only one suitcase."

"Yeah, but I don't like to break a sweat. How long are you going to be gone?"

"Not sure," I say.

"Have a good time," Roy says, punching my shoulder hard. "I'm sorry! I didn't mean to . . ."

"That's okay," I say, resisting the urge to rub my new injury.

Arlo steps forward. "Come on, son. Let's let her get to Louisiana in one piece. Have a good time, Stevie. I hope it's everything you want it to be."

I get in the van and Winston pulls away from his parking space, the one marked OWNER. We start to pass Horace and Ida, but Horace waves at us to stop. He wheels over to my side. "So you're off to Louisiana?"

"Yes."

"Ida and I wanted you to know that we're sure as heck sorry about what happened to the garden. That was a shame. The police should make those hoodlums fix it back."

"Thanks, Horace. And, Ida, thank you. I'll miss you."

Horace speaks for Ida. "We'll miss you too, Stevie."

"She has a bus to catch, folks," Winston says.

Everyone acts like they'll never see me again. Maybe they know something I don't. Maybe Winston is hoping I'll like my dad's family so much, I won't want to return.

When we near the garden, I look the other way. Winston yields to the oncoming traffic on I-35 and heads north toward Dallas.

Transplant

*To remove a plant from one area
and replant it in another*

Chapter Thirty-Eight

My bus passes through the East Texas city limits of Tyler and then of Longview. Pine trees border the highway. I doze awhile and awaken to find myself in Shreveport. The bus stops for new passengers. Then off we go again. I've had two seats to myself until this stop. Now a cute guy with a backpack sits next to me.

"Going to Baton Rouge," he says. "How about you?"

"Alexandria," I tell him.

"Alex," he says with a *k* sound at the end of the word. "They'll think you're a local if you call it that."

"Good to know," I say.

"What are you doing in Alex?"

"Visiting my aunt."

"I'm heading to L.S.U.," he says, as if I'd asked. "Starting in the summer to get some courses out of the way. Do you go to school?"

An image of a napping Mrs. Crump comes to mind. I smile.

"Did I say something funny?"

I shake my head. "I just finished eighth grade."

The guy pulls back and leans toward the window. "You look older."

Then he opens a book and reads.

AT THE BUS STATION in Alex, a knot forms in my stomach. I wonder if my aunt really wants to meet me.

"Have a good time with your aunt," the guy says as I step away.

"Good luck at L.S.U.," I call back to him. I think about Roy and his one dimple.

I glance around for a woman who might look something like my dad. But I may have to wait awhile.

Someone taps my shoulder. I swing around and a girl stares at me from head to toe. "You've got to be Stevie."

She has long brown hair and her skin is olive.

"Oh, my gosh!" the girl says. "You look just like me."

She's right. If she didn't have brown eyes, she could be my twin. There's the same small nose and mouth.

"Aren't you Stevie?" she asks.

I start to nod, but she's already hollering, "Momma, she's here!"

A lady with short brown hair and dark eyes like my father's walks over and spreads her arms out wide. "Stevie!"

She holds me tight and it feels so good. I haven't been hugged in a very long time. "Stevie, you are beautiful."

"Of course," the girl says. "She looks like me."

"But you must have your mother's eyes, right?" Aunt Teresa says. "Did she have blue eyes?"

So now I know. They never met Mom or me.

"I'm Megan. Your cousin. We're going to have a good time. I can't wait to introduce you to my friends and Brad. He's my boyfriend. Well, maybe I'd better not introduce you. You're too pretty. How old are you?"

"Thirteen."

"Good, you're too young for him. I'm seventeen."

Aunt Teresa grabs my bag and says, "Baby, I hope you like to eat, because you are going to have some good eating tonight."

"Momma made her famous potato salad," Megan says.

We walk to the car as they chirp like two magpies with every step. Aunt Teresa says, "Oh, my goodness. I can't believe this. My brother's child is here."

They talk so much that it takes me a while to realize we've made a few spins around the parking lot.

Aunt Teresa stops walking. "Oh, Lord, where did I park the car?"

When we pass the LEAVING ALEXANDRIA sign, Megan says, "You'd better warn Stevie about the men in our family."

"What's that?" Aunt Teresa asks.

"They're crazy, every one of them," Megan explains.

"Oh, that," Aunt Teresa says. "Well, just don't tell her about the bones buried in the backyard."

I must look shocked, because they glance at each other and crack up.

"So you're kidding?" I say slowly.

Megan exchanges looks with her mom and they both shake their heads. "No!"

"They're dog bones," Aunt Teresa explains. "Our family-dog cemetery plot."

We're driving past a sign that says WOODWORTH, and Aunt Teresa brakes so hard, she practically stops.

"They'll give you a ticket for sneezing in this place."

"Is this where you live?" I ask.

"No, we're three minutes away."

Then we pass a sign that reads FOREST HILL, NURSERY CAPITAL OF LOUISIANA. We take a left and drive over a railroad track. To the left is a little bank. To the right, a convenience store and the senior citizens center.

"Too bad you missed the Nursery Festival," Aunt Teresa says.

"I'll bet that's fun," I say.

"Fun? We'd have put you to work," Megan says.

"Don't mind my daughter. She has a warped sense of humor." Then she adds, "But we'd have put you to work for doggone sure."

When she says "for doggone sure," a prickle runs down my spine. My dad always said that.

Aunt Teresa slows the vehicle in front of a redbrick house with a sign in front that reads TANNER NURSERY. This must have been Dad's family home. A lot of large shrubs surround it, but I don't know what kind they are. A huge oak tree sits at the bend in the driveway.

The limbs are thick and far-reaching. One bows low, touching the ground. Rows and rows of black plastic pots of plants stretch out in the distance beyond the fence.

A lanky man with a purple L.S.U. baseball hat waves at us.

"That's your uncle Lloyd."

He heads our way, and Aunt Teresa rolls down the window. "This must be the famous Stevie," he says. "I'd give you a hug, but I'm sweaty. You're all we've talked about the whole week."

I don't know what to say. I just let the warmth of this moment pour over me. We get out of the car, and Uncle Lloyd lifts my suitcase from the trunk. "Is this all you have? You must want to run away from us quick."

A young boy comes out of the house. He wears a black top hat and a gold-satin-lined cape. He runs up to us and holds out a deck of cards.

"Pick a card," he demands. His narrow eyes slant a little on his moon-shaped face.

"Corbin, not now," Aunt Teresa says. "Remember our manners?"

Corbin looks up at Aunt Teresa.

"Introductions, remember?" she says.

He holds out his hand. "Hi, I'm Corbin Smith," he says in a thick voice. "Pick a card."

Everyone laughs.

"Later," Megan tells him.

"I'd like to pick a card," I say.

Megan shakes her head. "Oh, you don't know what you're starting."

Corbin shoves the deck in my face. The backs of the cards have umbrellas on them. "Don't let me see."

I select the seven of diamonds.

"Give it to me," Corbin says.

I do.

Corbin carefully turns the card upside down before slipping it into the deck. He shuffles, struggling as he steadies the cards against his chest. He settles on the dirt driveway and turns over each card until he reaches the queen of clubs. "Was this your card?" he asks.

I want to lie, but I shake my head a little.

"Just kidding!" he says. Then he turns over the seven of diamonds and stabs it with his finger. "This was your card."

I'm relieved. "Yes! Wow, you're talented, Corbin."

Corbin bows, straightens, and asks, "Aren't you going to clap?"

I clap and clap.

He bows again. Five times, then holds the deck out. "Pick a card."

Uncle Lloyd rescues me. "Let's go inside. Stevie must be exhausted. Corbin, take Stevie's bag to your sister's room. And then get your glasses on. You need to get used to wearing them."

Megan's room surprises me. It's pink and floral, like something a little girl who loves princesses would have, not a cool seventeen-year-old. Violet would love this room.

My face must reveal my thoughts, because she quickly says, "I've been meaning to redo this room for a while, but the nursery business hasn't been great lately. And I've been so busy, I haven't noticed, until now."

"It's pretty," I say. "I remember wishing I could have a pink room."

"When you were eight?" Megan asks.

We laugh. It feels as if we're old friends. Cousins.

"If you want to take a nap, I'll leave you alone."

"No, please don't. I'm not sleepy."

Her mouth breaks into a big grin and she plops on

her bed and sits cross-legged. "Good." She pats a spot across from her. "We've got lots to catch up on."

She pulls her yearbook off a shelf above her bed and begins to show me every boy she's ever had a crush on or who has asked her out on a date.

She points to one guy. "Not worth talking about the weather with."

She points to another. "The best kisser."

And another. "Bad breath."

And—"Sweet, sweet boy. I broke his heart."

An hour flies by. Aunt Teresa hollers, "Time for dinner! Get your little Smith behinds in here before the food gets cold."

We wash up.

"Tristen called," Megan says. "He's going to be late, but he said he'd be here before the blackberry cobbler."

We settle at the table in front of a platter piled high with fried chicken. Bowls of smothered okra, beans, and a salad of iceberg lettuce and sliced tomatoes. Mom didn't grow iceberg lettuce because she said it had no nutritional value. But this looks delicious.

All of a sudden it's quiet, for the first time since they picked me up at the bus station. I look around the table.

Everyone's eyes are closed and their heads are bowed. Then I hear Uncle Lloyd speak in a soft tone. "Father, we gather together . . ."

They're praying. I look at each one—*uncle, aunt, cousins.* It seems like I'm dreaming. I watch them until he says, "Amen."

They all say, "Amen." And then the chatter begins again.

"I'm getting a rabbit for Christmas," Corbin tells me, peering over his glasses.

"That's a long time from now," Aunt Teresa says, and from the way she says it, I can tell she's said a lot on the subject before.

"I'm going to pull a rabbit out of my hat."

"That's amazing," I tell him. "I can't do that."

"Are you a magician?"

"No," I say.

"Then why did you try to pull a rabbit out of your hat?"

"I didn't," I say.

"You'll never know unless you try," Corbin says.

"Well, that's true."

Corbin pulls a deck of cards from his lap and holds them up to me. "Pick a card."

"Corbin, put the cards away," Aunt Teresa says. "Remember? No magic tricks during dinner."

He puts the cards back in his lap.

There is talk about Megan's upcoming test. She's finishing her classes in summer school so that she can graduate early and start at L.S.U. in Alexandria. She wants to be a nurse.

Uncle Lloyd says to Megan, "I could sure use your help tomorrow."

"Daddy, I've got to study. Can't Tristen handle it?"

"Not tomorrow. Tristen has a big order to fill. We'll need more hands to get it done."

Aunt Teresa chimes in, "I'll be there, Lloyd. I think we can let Megan have the day to study."

"Thank goodness," Megan says. "This test is going to be a killer."

I'm trying to find the space to speak up, but they talk two at a time, barely breathing.

"I'll help," I say over the conversation.

They stop talking and look at me. "It's dirty work," Aunt Teresa says. "We didn't ask you here to work."

"I love plants. My parents had a garden. They grew flowers and herbs for a living."

Aunt Teresa's eyebrows shoot up. "They did? How funny."

I'm about to ask why that's funny when Uncle Lloyd says, "It's settled, then. Thank you, Stevie."

The front door swings open and a guy walks in. "Where's Momma's blackberry cobbler?" he asks.

Tristen is so good-looking, I feel myself blush. If he wasn't my cousin, I'd have a crush on him. A serious crush.

He walks over. "So this is Cousin Stevie?" He holds out his hand. I lift mine and he shakes hard. "Tristen Smith, marketing manager extraordinaire of Tanner Nursery."

Tristen has his family's knack for talking too. After he helps himself to a bowl of cobbler and vanilla ice cream, he reports on every moment of his day. He includes details, even changes his voice when he repeats what someone says. Listening to all of them is like watching a show. Like listening to Dad and his dinnertime stories about customers. They came to New Mexico from all over the world, and Dad could imitate every one of their accents.

That night while we're in bed, Megan tells me about her plans to be a nurse and how she and Brad will get married when she graduates. She falls asleep in mid-sentence. It's kind of funny, because she was speaking with such conviction, then off she goes to dreamland.

I slip out of bed and part the sheers on the window. Other than the light from an occasional car passing by on the highway, it's so dark. The moon is only a sliver. "Are you up there, Dad?" I whisper. "How could you keep something so wonderful from me?"

Chapter Thirty-Nine

UNCLE LLOYD DOESN'T TELL ME what time to get started, but I figure if he's like my parents, he goes out at dawn. I set my travel alarm for six a.m. Megan stirs when it goes off, but she keeps on sleeping. By the time I'm dressed, she awakens. "What are you doing up so early?"

"I told your dad I'd help him today."

She stretches her arms above her head. "Oh, Daddy is going to love you."

In the kitchen, Aunt Teresa is writing out checks by the light of a small lamp. She looks up at me. "My goodness, baby, I can't believe you're up with the chickens. How about some coffee and eggs?"

Even though I still haven't acquired a taste for it, I say, "Coffee sounds good."

"Cream and sugar?"

"Please."

"Just like your daddy."

It seems strange to hear my parents mentioned so naturally in less than twenty-four hours when they were rarely mentioned the whole time I was in Little Esther. I like it.

Uncle Lloyd comes in and pours himself a cup of coffee. He leans against the kitchen counter, and when he notices me, he says, "Up with the chickens, huh? We're going to get along just fine. Maybe you'll rub off on my daughter."

But just as he says that, Megan comes into the kitchen, grabs a honeybun out of the pantry, and waves to us as she leaves through the front door. "Bye! See you later!"

"Study hard, baby!" Uncle Lloyd hollers to her.

Megan waves again and drives off, the gravel crunching as she moves toward the highway.

Uncle Lloyd laughs and tells me, "Stevie, that's the

earliest I've seen Megan head out to study. You *are* going to be a good influence on her."

Aunt Teresa says, "Ah, Lloyd, she was afraid you were going to put her to work."

OUTSIDE, I FACE THE ROWS of potted plants. I don't know what they are, but I can tell there's grass where it shouldn't be.

Uncle Lloyd must notice too. "That grass needs pulling pretty bad out of those gardenias. Do you want to give it a try?"

"Sure."

I squat and begin to pull. Uncle Lloyd brings over a plastic stool. "Here, this will be better for your legs and back. You don't want to end up a humpback like me with two artificial knees."

I pull grass all morning. It's really hot outside. The air is thick and moist. I've never sweated so much in my life. And I'm not really working hard. The grass comes out of the pots with an easy tug. There are three workers on the other side of the field watering and pulling grass too.

Midmorning, Uncle Lloyd examines my task. "You're

a hard worker, Stevie. Why don't you kick off and enjoy the rest of the day?"

"It's only ten o'clock. I'm enjoying this."

"No way will I be responsible for taking away your contentment. I have some small plants that need transplanting into larger pots. Feel up to the chore?"

"I know how to do that."

"A worker with experience. Now how can I beat that?"

He guides me to an area where there are rows of one-gallon pots of Burford hollies and boxwoods. There's a potting area where I can stand, and containers of potting mix. I grab a handful and smell its sweet earthy scent. I think of the garden back in Taos and the one I started in Little Esther. The garden is ruined and the farm might as well be. Is there anything left of the life my parents started? I look across the nursery and see workers carrying pots to a truck, where Tristen leans against the bed, talking to his dad. Everyone is working hard. And I am too.

A few minutes later, I hear, "Want a permanent job?"

Tristen is grinning down at me. "Daddy says you

were out here before the rooster crowed. We appreciate it, but don't make the rest of us look bad." He laughs.

"I didn't see you this morning."

"I get up before the rooster crows too. Daddy and I drink our coffee on the back porch before dawn. We call it our business meeting. Go over the day's goals. Mostly we shoot the bull. Don't work too hard, cousin! See you in a few days in Florida. I've got a load to drive to Dallas." He walks away before I can ask him about Florida.

At lunch, Aunt Teresa comes out to the nursery. "Okay, baby, that's enough. Time to eat! And then I don't want you to step in this nursery for the rest of the day. Uncle Lloyd will take advantage of a good situation."

After I eat some leftover chicken and salad, I take a long bath. I'm so tired, my bones ache. And it feels good.

When I get dressed, I write a short letter to Frida apologizing for how wrong I'd been. I address it and ask Aunt Teresa if she will mail it for me when she picks Corbin up from Vacation Bible School.

She looks down at the envelope. "That's a pretty name—Frida."

That night, Megan tells me how she tried to keep her

mind on studying but there was that library boy. "He's supercute. He must live in the library. Every time I go, he's there, reading in the architecture section. How am I supposed to stay focused on my studies?"

"Maybe try the poetry section?"

"That's on the other side of the lib—Hey, that was funny, cuz! You're funny."

I smile, not because she said I was funny, but because she called me "cuz."

"Daddy says you worked like a dog. Is that true?"

"I like working with plants."

"Really?" She shakes her head. "Well, if you grew up around it..."

"I did."

"That's right. Did your parents have a nursery?"

"No, they grew flowers and herbs to sell at a stand on the side of Canyon Road."

"Now that sounds romantic."

I want to say that's what ended their lives, but I don't. And thank goodness Megan changes the subject.

"Want to know a secret?"

I nod eagerly.

"Corbin doesn't know this, but he's getting a rabbit for

his birthday. We'll be giving it to him in Florida next week."

"Are you going to Florida?"

"*We're* going. That means you too. Momma and Daddy rent a house for a week every summer in Pensacola. It's a blast. We go skiing and have crab boils, sleep late. I'll miss Brad, though."

"And Library Boy."

She sighs. "Oh, yes!" Then she cracks up and I join her.

Chapter Forty

ALL WEEK, I help in the nursery. I pull grass, transplant, water, fertilize. I love the routine. I love being here. At night I'm too tired to look at Mom's pictures. I decide to wait until I return to Little Esther.

There are so many things I want to ask Aunt Teresa about Dad, but I haven't had a chance yet. The family is so busy, and it's hard to get a word in during dinner conversations. At night, I think about everyone back at the Texas Sunrise Motel. And I wonder if they think of me too. Does Winston?

Then, this morning, I reach for the coffeepot and Aunt Teresa slaps her forehead. "Stevie, I forgot to tell you! Your grandfather called the other day."

"He did?"

"Yes, I'm sorry I didn't tell you. I was driving Corbin to Vacation Bible School and I couldn't talk long. He said he was checking to see if everything was going okay and if he needed to send you any money."

"For a ticket back to Little Esther?"

"Back to Little Esther? Do you already want to leave?"

"No," I say. And I mean it. I think. Still, I wish she had told me.

Aunt Teresa says, "Winston meant spending money. I told him we had you now and you didn't need a dime."

I stir the sugar into the coffee and watch it dissolve.

"You don't have to keep working," she says. "Although your uncle Lloyd thinks you hung the moon."

"I love working in the nursery." Here's my chance. I ask her, "Did Dad work in the nursery?"

"Growing up he did."

"Did he like it?"

Aunt Teresa looks down at her coffee cup, gets up, and dumps the remainder in the sink. She turns the faucet on and lets the water run into the cup. "No, he didn't like it much. Excuse me, baby, but I've got to get Corbin up and ready for Vacation Bible School."

When she leaves the room, I realize she's forgotten to turn the faucet off.

On Friday, I meet Brad. He comes over for dinner and to say good-bye to Megan, since they will be apart for "a whole seven days." He's different from what I thought he'd be. He's quiet, which I guess I should have guessed. How could he get in a word? When he does speak, he uses poor grammar. Still, Megan is crazy about him—I can tell. She teases him about the way he pronounces some words. He takes it well, but I wonder if he's embarrassed.

Later Megan tells me, "I know Brad isn't that smart, but he's sweet."

In bed, I think about what she says and decide I like Brad too. Then, for some reason, I fall asleep thinking about Roy.

Chapter Forty-One

ON THE WAY TO PENSACOLA, we play car karaoke, pretending the pen we pass around is a microphone. Megan begins singing a Lady Gaga song. And she's good.

When it's Corbin's turn, he says, "Pass."

"How about you, Stevie?" Megan says.

"Double pass," I say, although secretly I want to sing.

"Oh, come on," Megan says. "I'll bet you have a good voice. You share my gene pool."

"I guess you'll never know," I say.

Uncle Lloyd glances in the rearview mirror with a curled lip. "I believe that means it's my turn," he says with a soft drawl.

Megan groans. "Oh, brother. Elvis has entered the building."

Uncle Lloyd begins. *"Well, it's one for the money, two for the show…"*

We all crack up.

The game lasts a while, and then there is another round of chatter from the four. Even though they're funny to listen to, I'm hungry for a little slice of quiet. My thoughts drift and I wonder what movies Violet is watching this weekend. Maybe Roy is fishing with Arlo.

"Hel-lo? Earth to Stevie?" Megan waves her hand in front of my eyes.

"Oh, I'm sorry. What did you say?"

"Nothing that important," says Megan. "You were a million miles away. Were you thinking of some boy?"

My face burns. "Sorry."

"Don't apologize," Aunt Teresa says. "We're the ones who should be sorry. We could talk paint off a Cadillac." She points to a tall building. "Look, that's the Louisiana capitol."

"We're in Baton Rouge?"

Aunt Teresa taps Uncle Lloyd on the shoulder. "Take a swing through downtown so Stevie can see."

"Can we stop at Coffee Call?" Corbin asks.

"Good idea, Corbin. Love me some beignets," Uncle

Lloyd says. "We'll do that after we drive through downtown."

The whole time that they talk about the capitol and the Governor's Mansion, I'm looking for one thing: a giant on a unicycle. But of course I don't see him.

After the short tour, we head to Coffee Call. Megan starts to explain that a beignet is a deep-fried square doughnut with powdered sugar, but I interrupt her to tell her I already know. "My dad made them sometimes."

Inside Coffee Call, the sugary aroma filling the room pulls at my heart. I remember those special mornings Dad made the beignets: my birthday, Mom's, Christmas morning.

Jazz plays from the café sound system, and I think of Winston. We make our way to the back of the line and grab blue trays and mugs. Closer to the register are dispensers filled with café au lait and hot cocoa. I choose hot cocoa today. Uncle Lloyd asks for three orders of beignets.

At the table, Aunt Teresa tells me how when they were kids it was a big treat to come to Baton Rouge. "We'd always stop at Coffee Call, and Momma would let us eat as many beignets as we wanted. Oh, Lord, my belly would ache until the next day."

"Can I have as many as I want?" Corbin asks.

"No, sir," Aunt Teresa says.

"Why? You got to have as many as you wanted."

Aunt Teresa sighs. "Because my momma was a foolish person who didn't think there were any rules."

I realize she's talking about Dad's mom too. My grandmother, another person I'll never know.

"When did she die?" I ask.

Aunt Teresa runs her finger around the rim of her mug. "When I was in high school and your dad was about twelve. Oh, it killed him when she died. Your dad was especially close to her. They were a lot alike. And when she died, Daddy was hard on him."

Uncle Lloyd gives Aunt Teresa a stern look.

"Oh, don't listen to me," she says. "I talk too much."

But I don't want her to shut up. I want to hear everything she knows about Dad.

Chapter Forty-Two

PENSACOLA MAKES ME THINK of the beach dream I've remembered my entire life. Maybe because of seeing the beach, I'm remembering more details in the dream—the white sand, the seagulls, the huge waves splashing the shore. Driving to the cabin, I hear the guitar song playing in my ear. It's so clear now, a familiar tune, but I don't remember the words. I don't realize I'm humming it until Aunt Teresa announces, "'Blackbird.' I love that Beatles song."

Somehow I know she's right, although it's only now that I do remember the song being a part of the dream. I remember the man holding my hand as we walked near the edge of the ocean. He pointed at my small footprints next to his big ones and said, "Watch the waves!" The ocean spilled over and made little pools in our prints, then the next time it washed over them, they disappeared. Now I wonder if maybe it really happened. Maybe we were here or at another beach. Especially since Aunt Teresa loved that song. Maybe Dad did too.

Corbin is talking about the hermit crabs he plans to find on the beach, and Megan is telling me about a family who rented the cabin next door to them last year. "They had the cutest son."

We pass some houses on tall stilts. At the end of the road, we pull into a driveway and park under the carport below the cabin.

"Home away from home," Aunt Teresa says. "Everyone grab something. The beach has to wait until we are unpacked."

We climb the stairs to a door with a temporary sign that reads THE CRAZY SMITHS.

They don't seem to notice, but I giggle when I see it.

"Oh," Megan says, "the sign?"

I nod.

"We've been coming here the same time every summer since I was a baby. The landlady knows us well."

The front door takes a good shove to open. Uncle

Lloyd says that's because the wood expands and shrinks, depending on the weather.

We walk straight into a spacious living area with two couches and chairs. A long dining room table is at one end in front of an ocean-view window. The cabin smells salty and a little like fried fish. The other rooms are cozy, including the kitchen, where a small table for two sits against the wall.

Megan and I share a room again. Uncle Lloyd and Aunt Teresa take the other room. The guys will crash on the sleeper sofas.

"Tristen will be here in a few days," Aunt Teresa says. "In time for your magic show, Corbin."

"My birthday magic show," Corbin says.

"It's your birthday?" Megan has a fake surprised expression. "Really? I almost forgot."

Corbin's shoulders drop. "You almost forgot my birthday?"

"Never!" she says. "Just wanted to make sure you hadn't forgotten."

"Never!" Corbin says. He digs in his pockets and pulls out the deck. "Pick a card," he tells me.

And for the eighteenth time since I got in the car this morning, I do.

While we unpack, Meagan says, "I know we all spoil Corbin, but he's special in a lot of ways. Our family wouldn't be the same without him."

"He's a great little guy," I tell her.

After our dinner of chicken-salad sandwiches, Uncle Lloyd takes us on a boat ride. The sun hangs low in the sky, as if it's ready to dip into the water. When he stops the boat, Corbin leans over and stares. "After I learn to pull a rabbit out of my hat, I'm going to pull out a fish."

We all laugh.

"Corbin," Uncle Lloyd says, "you are an original."

"That can be my magician name. The Great Original Magician, Corbin Smith."

I take a big breath. I want to inhale this moment and let it fill me until I almost burst from the happiness of it all.

Chapter Forty-Three

THE LAST FOUR DAYS at the beach have been great. Horace and Ida enter my thoughts a lot. I sure hope they can get here one day. Pensacola would be a nice place for them to have their honeymoon. I decide to make a list of all the places they might want to go if they ever do. I write down names of hotels and restaurants. I write down the place where we watched a school of dolphins swim by and where you can rent out giant beach umbrellas. Even as I write these things, I know Horace and Ida will need help getting around. If I were older, I'd take them here and anywhere they'd want to go.

It's Corbin's birthday. We've sung "Happy Birthday" a zillion times, beginning with his pancake breakfast. He should be excited about his magic show tonight, but he seems nervous. Whenever anyone mentions the show, he gets quiet and pushes at the nose bridge of his glasses. When I see him sitting on the steps outside the front door, I join him. "What's wrong, Corbin?"

"I can't pull a rabbit out of the hat," he whispers. "I'm going to mess up."

I'm confused because I thought he didn't know anything about the rabbit. He must have found out. Why else would he have planned the trick?

So I ask, "How are you going to pull a rabbit out of the hat? I thought you weren't getting one until Christmas?"

"Mom gave me a rabbit."

Now I'm really confused.

Corbin leaves the room and comes back with a stuffed rabbit.

I sigh. "Of course!" There's still going to be a surprise. "Of course you can pull a rabbit out of the hat. You just have to practice. Do you want me to help?"

He shakes his head. "No, a magician never shares his secrets." He walks away.

A couple of hours later, Tristen arrives. After updating his dad on the Dallas delivery, he motions for me to follow him. We go downstairs to his truck. He lifts a cage sitting on the floorboard. A white rabbit with pink eyes twitches its nose.

"Okay, here's what I need from you, cousin. We're going to hide the cage behind the ice chest in the mudroom. When Corbin begins his magic show, slip downstairs and get the rabbit. Bring it upstairs. When Corbin pulls the stuffed rabbit out of his hat, say, 'Ta-da!' and hold up the real rabbit."

I feel giddy, like I'm one of Santa's helpers.

"Are you up to it?"

"Yes!"

"Awesome."

"I can't wait!"

"It'll be great. I hope you don't mind that I asked you. It's just he would notice anyone in the family that was missing."

When he says that, my stomach sinks. I guess I'd started to feel like part of the family. But I straighten my shoulders and follow him inside. This is Corbin's day.

And nothing will keep me from making it anything but the best birthday ever.

AND IT IS the best birthday ever. Corbin is doing the "pick a card" trick when I go downstairs for the rabbit. The rabbit looks back at me with those pink eyes. "Hey, Mr. Rabbit. You're about to meet the best little guy for a friend. Be good to him."

When I sneak upstairs with the cage, Corbin stands in the middle of the room with everyone gathered around. I stand back, near the front door, so he won't see me. He asks Megan to pick a card. "I've already picked a card. We've all had two turns. Let's see another trick."

"Yes, Corbin," Aunt Teresa says, "pull a rabbit out of the hat."

Corbin's shoulders let down, and I'm remembering our talk on the stairs. "I don't think I'm ready."

I rest the cage down and step forward. "You'll never know unless you try. Remember you told me that when I met you?"

Corbin takes a deep breath and pulls his hat off. He puts his handkerchief over the hat and shows everyone.

"See?" he says. "No rabbit."

"There's not a hare in sight," says Tristen. He winks at me.

I walk to the cage and open it. I pick up the rabbit, who is not at all happy about it. He scratches my arm so hard, I have to bite my lip so that I don't cry out. The rabbit wiggles from my hold.

Corbin removes his handkerchief and pulls the stuffed rabbit out of the hat. "Ta-da!"

Everyone except Corbin looks in my direction. I squat, but the rabbit is hopping away. He hops, hops, hops until he's under a chair.

Aunt Teresa claps. Corbin bows and bows.

I block one end and Megan blocks the other. She bends down and pulls the rabbit out from under the chair. "Gotcha!"

But just as Megan starts to stand, the rabbit scratches her. "Ouch!" She lets go. He hops and hops around the room. Everyone is laughing, trying to catch him, except for Corbin, who is still standing in the same spot. When the rabbit moves to the side of the couch, Uncle Lloyd heads in the rabbit's direction, but he trips and falls over a sofa arm. Tristen corners the rabbit near the coffee table.

The rabbit slips away, escaping through his open legs. Finally, the rabbit stops when he reaches Corbin's feet. We all freeze. We're afraid to move.

It's now that Corbin notices.

He squeals and picks up his new pet. "I did it! I made a rabbit appear! I'm magic!"

Chapter Forty-Four

WE'VE BEEN AT THE BEACH for five days and we've just finished the annual crawfish-boil dinner. I've been waiting for an opportunity to catch Aunt Teresa alone. I want to ask a lot of questions. The newspapers have been thrown away along with the crawfish shells and corncobs. Megan says I'm now an official Cajun since I've learned to appreciate sucking the crawfish heads.

Corbin's attention to his rabbit has given us a break from picking cards. He's sitting on the floor next to the cage, watching his new pet, Lucky Dog.

Tristen stands and cracks his knuckles. "Ready for me to defend my King of Charades title?"

"Your what?" I ask.

"You've never played charades?" Megan is clearly baffled.

"No way, cuz!" Tristen shakes his head in mock shame. "Deprived!"

"I'll bet Stevie has played chess," Aunt Teresa says.

How did she know?

"Your daddy liked chess when he was a bitty boy," she says. "Momma taught him. She'd take Sheppard to play with the old men at the country club in Alex. Made my daddy so mad. We weren't even members. We didn't have that kind of money. But that didn't stop Momma when she got a notion in her head. Remember I told you she didn't believe in rules? Then Sheppard went on to play in school. Won a lot of championships. You should see the trophies."

"Yeah," Tristen says. "He must have been something else. He won all over the state."

Megan laughs. "One of his trophies says 'Gumbo Chess King'!"

"Really?" I never knew Dad had won titles or competed in school.

"Trip to the attic," Megan says. "That's where Uncle Sheppard's trophies are. Add it to the list, Daddy."

Using his finger, Uncle Lloyd writes in the air. "Got it!" Then he says, "Yeah, your daddy played all the time until that kid moved into town. Whiz kid. Beat Sheppard bad with that funny move. I can't remember what they called it. What was it called, Tristen?"

"Cherub mate?" I ask at the same time Tristen says it.

"You know the story?" he asks.

I'd always thought the tattoo on my dad's belly represented the game that won the farm.

"Do you need to know the rules?" Tristen is standing now.

"Chess? No, I know those rules by heart."

"No, cousin. Charades." Tristen is punching his fist into his other palm, clearly ready to defend his title.

"But I've never played."

"It's easy, easy," Megan begins.

Tristen interrupts, shaking his finger at Megan. "Ah-ah-ah. You'd better let me explain. You need to learn from an honest person."

"Hey, now!" Megan puts her hands on her hips, pretending to be offended.

Corbin pops up from the floor and moves across the room until he stands directly in front of me. He rotates his fist like he's cranking a camera. "This means movie." He goes on to show the gestures for *book* and *TV show*.

Tristen explains, "You have to get the others to guess which title you're acting out."

"You can't talk," Megan adds.

"And that is why Megan always loses," Tristen says. "She can't keep her mouth shut."

Megan throws her hands in the air. "Kill Tristen! Add that to the list, Daddy!"

Aunt Teresa is taking inventory in the refrigerator. "Don't forget to add milk to the list."

We crack up.

"Oh, Momma," Megan groans.

Aunt Teresa turns around. "What?"

I study them. They're laughing and talking at the same time. They're like a well-fitting glove. And in that moment, I want so badly to be a part of them.

Chapter Forty-Five

THE CHARADES GAME has been going on an hour, and there's no end in sight. Aunt Teresa is the only one who isn't playing, and I realize this is my chance to be alone with her.

"I fold," I tell the rest.

"Aw, you're doing so good, too," Megan says.

"No, you're the Crazy Smiths. Can't beat you."

"She's got us pegged," Uncle Lloyd says.

"My turn!" Tristen holds his open palms together.

"Book!" yells Corbin.

In the kitchen, Aunt Teresa is writing something on a notepad. "I'm finishing the grocery list for the last few days. We're already out of snack food."

I've eaten a mountain of corn chips.

She pushes the chair across from her with her foot. "Tired of charades?"

I sit. "I'm better at chess. But I haven't played in a long time."

"Yeah, your daddy was something."

"Why did Dad leave Louisiana?"

"You don't know?" Aunt Teresa studies my face, chin to forehead.

I shake my head.

"Oh, Stevie, your parents must have kept so much from you."

This hits a nerve. Even though I've been feeling this way since I left New Mexico, I say, "They just didn't like to talk about their pasts."

"Obviously."

"I was taught that today is what matters." A lump gathers in my throat.

She raises her eyebrows.

"We were happy." I hear the choke in my voice. I miss them so much. I want her to know what great parents they were. They were perfect. Well, maybe not perfect, but almost. We were a trio. It bothers me that Aunt Teresa doesn't see what I know deep in my heart. But I also know that if I've learned anything since leaving New Mexico, it's that my parents had secrets.

Aunt Teresa lets out a big sigh and looks toward the water. "Your dad didn't want to take over the nursery. Sheppard was going to be a chess champion. In many ways, I think he did it because of Momma. He wanted to make her proud of him, even beyond the grave. And for a while, it looked like his dream was going to come true. Until he lost that game to that kid from Kenner. He lost something else when he lost that game. He lost his confidence. He'd lose over foolish plays. He'd lose one minute into the game. It was devastating to watch. Our dad told him the writing was on the wall. He might as well take up his destiny.

"The nursery needed him. Daddy needed him. I was married to Lloyd and we were living in Norfolk. Lloyd was in the navy. That was his dream. When your dad took off, Lloyd didn't reenlist. He came back to Louisiana with me and helped Daddy with the nursery. I don't like remembering this, but I was mad at Sheppard. Real mad. He called once when he heard Daddy had died. We got into it big-time. I told him he was selfish and spoiled.

And when he didn't come back home for Daddy's funeral, I didn't think I'd ever forgive him."

"Did he ever call back?"

Aunt Teresa taps the pen on the tablet. "No. That was the last time we spoke."

A burst of laughter comes from the other room. "That is not a title!" I hear Megan yell.

Aunt Teresa touches my arm. "Look, you can blame me as much as him for our separation. We wasted a lot of years. Eighteen years. When I found out...what happened, I was devastated. I guess I always thought there'd be time for us to make up and get on with things. But now it's too late. Then I learned about you and I thought, *Here's my second chance.* I can't make it up to my brother, but I can have a relationship with his child. My niece."

I'm not sure what to say. It's all so much to take in.

"So he taught you to play chess? I'm surprised he still played."

"He won our farm in a chess game." I say it proudly. I want her to know Dad wasn't a loser.

"That's something," she says, and I can tell she's impressed. "Stevie, Uncle Lloyd and I have been talking since you've come to visit. We want you to live with us. We all love you. You're so easy to love. And you're family."

Her words cause a lump in my throat. I can't speak.

"Don't answer now, but think about it. Please."

We reach for each other at the same time, and she gives me a squeeze. "I'm a good hugger," she says.

"You are," I manage to say without crying. "Do you mind if I go for a walk on the beach?"

"By yourself?"

I nod.

"Don't go too far, and take a flashlight."

Before leaving the kitchen, I say, "I thought Winston would have called more often."

Aunt Teresa looks embarrassed. "I'm so sorry. Forgive my ditzy brain. He did call. Three times since you've come to us. He just wanted to know if you needed anything. And, of course, you don't."

How do I tell her I needed to know that?

Aunt Teresa follows me through the charades room. Megan hollers, "Want some company?"

I shake my head, and my aunt says, "I think Stevie needs some time to herself."

"Oh," Megan says softly.

An awkward quiet falls over the room. I walk through the front door and take the stairs down to the landing.

It's dusk, and I think about how Mom grew quiet at this time of day. Maybe she was thinking of my grandfather. I'm thinking of him now. Winston is usually doing the books at this time or taking in late arrivals.

I step on something sharp and discover an oyster shell sticking up in the sand. My thoughts turn to pearls and how the magic of time turns a grain of sand into something round and hard, so solid it could never return to a grain of sand. Maybe that's what happened with Mom and Winston. A hurt that grew over the years into something round and hard. There was no returning. And that's sad, because if my parents taught me anything, it was that hope exists in any situation. The way they continued to water a wilted plant, the way they weathered the days when no one stopped by the stand. They taught me hope.

The sun is now a pinkish-orange ball skimming the gulf. I think about Winston and how he cut Mom off from the world because he didn't want to lose her when my grandmother died. Mom ended up doing exactly what he feared most. Maybe Winston didn't want to let me into his life because he didn't want to be hurt again. He'd lost me once before. My body feels heavy moving through the sand. I walk closer to the tide and let the water reach my toes. When I turn around, I realize I've broken my promise to Aunt Teresa. I've walked a long way from the cabin. So I head back.

Soon, I notice a group of people moving in my direction. It's my family. They must have been worried about me. The heaviness I felt just moments ago gives way to a warmth traveling all the way up to my head. They care about me, maybe even love me, like Aunt Teresa said. They're too far for me to hear what they're saying, but I can hear Uncle Lloyd's voice and I figure he's telling one of his funny Cajun jokes. It must have been awful, because now I hear Aunt Teresa say, "Lloyd, shame on you!"

For the first time since my parents died, I know where I belong. My body feels lighter and I move quickly toward them. My family, the Crazy Smiths. I'll miss each one of them.

Chapter Forty-Six

"Texas Sunrise Motel." The voice is familiar.

"Roy?"

"The one and only. Hey, is this that deserter? The girl who ran away to Louisiana?"

"The one and only," I say. "Where's Winston? He's okay, isn't he?"

"He stepped away for a couple of hours. I'm officially in charge of the Bloomin' Office."

"How's your dad?"

"He's fine. He's at the movies."

I wonder why he went without Roy, but I ask, "How's Violet?"

"She's at the movies."

I connect the dots. "Wait a minute—what?"

"Mmm hmm," Roy says. "You got it."

"A lot has happened in two weeks."

"Yep. A pipe broke, three rooms flooded, discovered a leak from the roof, and an old yellow cat showed up that doesn't seem to want to leave. Winston gripes, but I've caught him feeding it. You'd better get back before the Texas Sunrise Motel falls apart."

I'm wishing Roy would say he misses me, but I remember how he acted funny when I said good-bye.

Then Roy says, "And you need to get back so I can teach you to brake on those skates."

"Would you leave Winston a message for me?"

"Sure. Hold on. Let me get a pen."

I'm waiting and waiting. Then Roy speaks into the phone. "Sorry, I'm still looking."

"Winston keeps the pens in the middle drawer," I tell him.

"Thanks!"

I hear the drawer screech open, a sound I've heard a thousand times before.

"Okay," Roy says. "I'm ready."

"Ask Winston to send me a ticket home."

And even though we're hundreds of miles away from each other, I hear the pen drop.

A FEW DAYS LATER, I still haven't received the ticket and Winston hasn't bothered to call. When I mention it to Aunt Teresa, she jokes, "Well, maybe he changed his mind. Maybe he wants you to stay with us."

But this isn't funny, not to me, anyway. The minute I heard Roy's voice, I knew I missed him and everyone else at the motel, including Winston. I can't get that picture out of my mind of him feeding a cat on the sneak and then complaining that the cat is still hanging around. Winston is not as tough as he wants everyone to think.

All day, I think about how what happened four months ago has changed the rest of my life. Even now while we sit around the dinner table and everyone is chattering, I think about it. Uncle Lloyd and Tristen argue over who almost caught the biggest fish. Megan is telling her mom that she's so confused about Brad, and Corbin is talking to me about Lucky Dog. I'm barely listening. My thoughts are far away in Texas.

Aunt Teresa is serving us each a piece of coconut pie when the neighbors' dogs go to barking. Soon we hear the crunching of the gravel outside and a knock at the door.

Everybody gets quiet, and I notice they're all looking at me. Aunt Teresa says, "Stevie, will you get the door?" Which seems strange for her to ask me to do, but maybe she knows something I don't. Maybe someone is delivering my ticket.

I walk across the room, open the door, and find Winston standing there.

He doesn't say anything.

I don't say anything.

Then I lean into his chest and wrap my arms around him. Winston's arms form a ring around my body. We're hugging, and it's like we're saying hello for the very first time.

Blooming

Flowering, flourishing, prospering

Chapter Forty-Seven

"WE'RE GOING TO TAKE a little detour," Winston says an hour into our journey back to Little Esther. There's a lot of silence between Winston and me. That's okay. We're not the Crazy Smiths. We're quiet people. But we talk some too.

"I like your aunt," Winston says. "And Lloyd seems like a good person."

"He is."

I think Winston is trying to figure out if something went wrong, something that would cause me to go back with him. And of course nothing did go wrong, but I'll let Winston just wonder about that for now.

Aunt Teresa knew Winston was coming. While I packed my suitcase, she said she called Winston shortly after I told her I was going back to Little Esther. She said he didn't say a word for a good while. Then he asked how long we'd be in Pensacola, because he wanted to come for me himself.

We're about to cross the Florida state line. Good-bye, Florida. "What's the detour?"

"I want to stop in New Orleans to see an old friend."

A Cajun music station is on the radio. I can tell the song is zydeco, because that's what Uncle Lloyd listened to at the nursery. I wouldn't have known that two weeks ago. Just like I wouldn't ever have guessed in a million years that Winston would drive all the way to Pensacola to get me.

A couple of hours pass. We cross the long bridge over Lake Pontchartrain and enter the New Orleans city limits.

"Did you ever play here?"

"Oh, yeah. Quite a bit. It was hard being on the road, leaving my family, but this city kind of grabs hold of your soul and won't let go."

I wonder if we're going to a jazz club, but we pass the French Quarter exit sign and cross the Mississippi River. The sun is high in the sky, bouncing light off the dark water. An old steamboat with a red paddle wheel spits water, making its way along the riverbank. When we reach the other side of the bridge, we turn off the main road onto a side street. Then we pull up in front of a nursing home. Winston parks the van. "Hop out. There's someone I want you to meet."

Winston opens the side door and pulls out a guitar case.

"You play the guitar?"

"A little."

We pass a few older people sitting in rocking chairs on the porch and go inside. The place smells like bleach and a sour mop.

A lady behind the desk at the entrance asks, "Can I help you?" Then she smiles. "Oh, it's you again. Here to see Jack? Room Forty-Three down the east hallway."

Winston thanks her, and we walk down the hallway to the right. The doors are decorated with wreaths and craft projects that look like little kids made them. Some have pictures of people taped all over.

Room 43 is midway down the hall. Winston knocks.

"Come on in this place," a gravelly voice calls out.

Winston opens the door.

"Hey, cat!" the old black guy says. He's sitting up in bed, watching the news on TV. Pointing the remote toward the screen, he turns the power off. "Who's this pretty thing you have with you, Winston?"

"This is Stevie, my granddaughter."

I've never heard him call me that before. I like the way it sounds coming out of his mouth.

"What brings you to town? It's not the Jazz Fest already?"

"No, that was last month. I was picking up Stevie. She was in Pensacola with her aunt's family. Taking her back to Little Esther."

The man faces me. "Oh, you poor pitiful thing. Little Esther, where they watch the grass grow."

"Stevie, meet Jack. We used to play a few tunes together."

"Only about a thousand or two." Jack stretches his right arm my way and we give each other a good handshake.

He gives me a long, hard look. "She's got Dovie's eyes, don't she?"

"And her mother's," Winston says.

Jack stares at the guitar. "You gonna play me a tune?"

"I've got a song or two left in me," Winston says.

"Let's hear it now."

Winston opens the case and pulls out the guitar. "Stevie, can you pull that chair up for me?"

I scoot the chair so that he's close to Jack's bedside. For a couple of minutes, he plucks the strings and tunes the instrument. Then he begins to play. The music is familiar. When he sings the first words, I remember the song and a whole lot more.

Blackbird singing in the dead of night.

I remember the beach and the man with curly hair.

Take these broken wings and learn to fly.

I remember him holding my hands and leading me into the water. "See the waves?" he said. "Jump." I remember my mother laughing and singing with the man. Singing this song.

Winston's voice is gentle and smooth. When he finishes, Jack says, "That's real nice."

Winston catches me rubbing my eyes. He doesn't have to ask. I see the question on his face. He's wondering if I remember.

We soon tell Jack good-bye and leave.

On the porch next to the rockers, I ask, "We went to the beach with Mom, didn't we?"

"Yes, we did." I can tell he's pleased.

"I thought it was a dream. Were we in Pensacola?"

"Galveston," he says.

Back on the other side of the river, Winston takes me to the French Quarter, and for the second time that month I eat beignets. This time at Café Du Monde. There's music pouring into the streets and people walking everywhere. When we go to cross to Jackson Square, we step back, because coming down the road is a guy on a unicycle. He is tall, very tall. He breezes by us so fast.

"Did you see that?" Winston says. His voice is an octave higher. "That guy must be seven feet tall!"

We watch the man's back until he turns onto another street. Everyone is stopping and gawking. I'm reminded of the knitting lady's words: *Everyone always stops for a giant on a unicycle.* All these months, I thought about seeing him with that red scarf around his neck, holding a stack of flyers in his hands. But today there are no flyers and he's wearing a blue T-shirt. That shouldn't be a surprise, because it feels like it's a hundred degrees out-side. Still, I'm excited about seeing him and I can't help thinking it's a sign.

On the drive to Little Esther, I want to ask so many questions, but I hold off. The details will spill out from Winston a little at a time. Like Mom's photographs, I want the stories to unfold and I want to savor each bit. We have a whole lifetime to catch up. There is one question that I want answered now, though.

"Winston?"

"Hmm?"

"What's in Room Twelve?"

He pauses a long time. For a minute, I think he's not going to answer me. Then he says, "My life."

AT THE MOTEL, something is different. Then I realize it's the garden. A bench now sits under the arbor. There are marigolds and periwinkles. Lots of marigolds and peri-winkles. I smile. Roy must have had something to do with this. They aren't perennials, but I love the garden. Maybe that's what seeing the giant on the unicycle in New Orleans meant. Even if life doesn't turn out exactly like we thought it would, it can still be wonderful. Just because Mom and Dad died, it doesn't mean my life is over. They would want me to be happy.

Marigolds and periwinkles. "Who did this?" I ask.

"Everyone. Roy, Arlo, Violet," Winston says. "Even Horace and Ida helped with the watering. And Mercedes planted some seeds around that arbor. Morning glories, I think. They aren't blooming yet. We started the day after you left."

Then, as we drive up next to it, I see a patch of phlox that has reseeded from the ones Mom planted. Their pink pom-poms wave to me in the breeze as if they're welcoming me back. Back home.

Chapter Forty-Eight

ROY AND I are almost finished with Mrs. Crump's yard. Then we're going to tackle Violet's. Australia will have to wait. I used the money for gardening tools at Gavert's. Nancy gave me a great discount.

I've been home a month and during that time Roy and I have become guerrilla gardeners. We show up, plant, and tidy the yards. Nancy provides all our plantings. She knows the people here who can't afford her service.

The motel garden hasn't gotten us more customers, but the ones who do stop seem happier. Some of them even walk out to the garden and, if the yellow cat we call Buttercup is not stretched out there, they sit on the bench under the arbor. Mercedes's morning glories have started to bloom. Sometimes I want to say to the people sitting there, *Do you know there's a love story tangled in that vine?*

Arlo and Violet have become quite the couple, but these days the love story I like most is Horace and Ida, who are finally on their honeymoon. Winston tracked down the driver who drove the bus for them years ago when they were dating. The one who helped them elope. Seems only natural he'd be the one to take them to Pensacola. Winston took care of all the expenses, including a room with a beach view.

The sun is high in the sky. Roy and I are sweating buckets. I thought Mrs. Crump would have heard Roy mowing the lawn, but she hasn't come out of the house yet. Then I realize it's ten till two. Naptime. Soon after the clock strikes two, she comes out of the house and, from the porch, surveys what we've done. "Oh, my! What did I do to deserve this kindness?"

After she goes back inside, Roy says, "You're right. She's kind of cool, isn't she?" He says it with that one-dimple grin that always makes my legs wobbly.

Winston picks us up in his van. He told Mrs. Crump last week that I'd be going to the high school this fall. I asked him what she said. "Actually, she looked relieved. Or sleepy. I'm not sure which."

Frida never wrote me back, but I didn't expect her to. Her mom was right. She'll be starting school with me this fall. I figure she might need someone around to help her with geography. I did receive three letters, though. One was from Aunt Teresa inviting me back next summer and any other time that I'd like. Megan's letter was short. She and Brad broke up. "It was all because of the library boy." She just couldn't get him out of her mind.

The third letter, which I received yesterday, was from Paco. He sent me a check for $784.54. He told me that the money for the farm was in a special account waiting for me. This was a refund from something else.

He wrote,

While going through the last of your parents' possessions, I found six bus tickets. They were for this summer and for two destinations—Dallas and, a week later, Alexandria, Louisiana. Apparently they were planning two trips with you. I'm surprised your dad didn't mention it to me, since I'm sure I would have been asked to look

after the farm while you were away. Because of the
circumstances, I was able to get a full refund. I hope
you'll enjoy the money. Have some fun with it. I think
your parents would like that. Write to me and let me
know how you're doing. I'll always be here for you.

Love, Paco

My parents were planning on visiting my grandfather and Aunt Teresa after all. The tickets prove it. Although knowing the trip would never happen for them
makes me sad, knowing they planned it makes me happy.
I decide I'll wait for the right moment to show Paco's letter to Winston. Maybe for his birthday next week. I'll
make him chicken-fried steak and mashed potatoes
with cream gravy. I'll wrap the letter in pretty paper and
tie it with a bow. I'll make a copy and send it to Aunt
Teresa too.

On the way back to the motel, Roy and Winston talk
about the Dallas Cowboys' upcoming season. I stare out
the window. The weather is hot and dry. It's a good thing
I chose plants that don't need much watering or fussing.

I'm thinking about my plans for Violet's yard when I

see a guy walking along the highway in the distance. Even though he's way off, I notice his blue backpack. I wonder if Dad walked along this very stretch of road when he was passing through Little Esther. The guy is still ahead of us, but for a moment I imagine him as Dad. Then I see Mom walking next to him, her blond curls blowing in the wind and her camera around her neck.

Their images are so clear that I press my hand against the window, yearning for them to look my way. My reflection in the glass stares back at me. Then I realize—*I am there*. And they are here. After all that has happened these last few months, I believe this. I'm like that seedling in the spot between where the sweetheart trees once grew. Despite everything, I'm certain it's growing, reaching toward the clouds, branching out to all the places they once had been.

Acknowledgments

My editor and I worked together for two years before ever seeing each other. Less than twenty-four hours after we'd finally met, she kindly sat on my suitcase so that I could lock it. Christy, you are always helping me get to the next place. When you think about it, that's kind of astonishing after twenty years of working together. Thank you for your support and belief in my work.

Thank you, Amy, for valuing my career. Thank you for your honesty and integrity. I value you.

Thank you to my Writing Retreat pals—Kathi, Jeanette, Rebecca, and Lola—for your encouragement and wisdom. Much gratitude to Jenny and Charlotte, too, for friendship, words, and commas. Thanks to Jane, Martha, and Amanda for reading a few early chapters. Thanks, Dewayna, for a glimpse into your beautiful work. Thank you to the good folks at Halbert's Nursery.

My parents grew up in Forest Hill and worked in nurseries. They shared those years through their stories. As a writer and their daughter I'm grateful for that. And for my mom and grandfather who passed down their love for gardening to me.

Every writer needs a gifted first reader. My daughter has been mine since she was seven. Thank you, thank you, Shannon.

And thank you, Jerry, for being the kind of husband who twenty-two years ago gave me a year to just write. You drive me crazy, but I love you.